The Expendables

The Expendables

Stories by Antonya Nelson

The University of Georgia Press

Athens and London

c. 1

© 1990 by Antonya Nelson
Published by the University of Georgia Press
Athens, Georgia 30602
All rights reserved

Set in 10 on 14 Trump Mediaeval
The paper in this book meets the guidelines
for permanence and durability of the Committee on
Production Guidelines for Book Longevity of the
Council on Library Resources.

Printed in the United States of America

94 93 92 91 90   5 4 3 2 1

Library of Congress Cataloging in Publication Data

Nelson, Antonya.
    The expendables : stories / by Antonya Nelson.

      p. cm.
    ISBN 0-8203-1156-1 (alk. paper)
    I. Title.
    PS3564.E428E97 1990
    813'.54—dc20   89-31444
                                                  CIP

British Library Cataloging in Publication Data available

For Susan and Julie,

and for Robert and Jade

Acknowledgments

The author and publisher gratefully acknowledge the following publications in which these stories, sometimes in earlier versions, have previously appeared:

Borderline: "You Boys Be Good"
Indiana Review: "Substitute"
The North American Review: "Dog Problems"
Other Voices: "Looking for Tower Hall"
Playgirl: "Maggie's Baby," "Helen in Hollywood"
Prairie Schooner: "Mud Season"
Quarterly West: "Cold Places"
Short Story Review: "Affair Lite"

"Slickrock to Bedrock" was originally published in *Esquire* under the title "Downstream"; "Listener" was a Nelson Algren Award winner and published in the *Chicago Tribune*; "The Expendables" first appeared in the anthology *American Fiction 88*; "You Boys Be Good" was selected for the PEN Syndicated Fiction Project; and "Looking for Tower Hall" and "You Boys Be Good" were winners of *Tucson Weekly*'s annual fiction contest.

The author thanks the Illinois Arts Council for its support.

Contents

The Expendables

Listener

"Why did you stop?" her husband asks. His hand had lifted, as it did involuntarily, while she was reading, but as soon as she'd quit it had dropped back into his lap, lifeless. "Julia?" he says, and though his hands are both peacefully draped on his lap, his voice holds the most minor of tremors, perhaps perceptible only by his wife. "Julia, is there something . . . ?"

"It's just that man again."

Averil's hand rises when he hears her voice. It flits to his collar, to his ear, his nose, a pattern his hand has etched into any space Averil inhabits. He is blind, and when he hears his wife's voice, when his hand senses her voice on the air, he must check the other senses rapidly. He is here, they seem to tell him, he fills a shirt, a body; he can enclose himself with his hands.

"Next door?" he says, gently.

"Across the way." Not an alley, just a brief ten-foot space between windows. "I can't get used to apartments," she says, rising to pull the shades. The room shrinks, the light dulls. "But I can't stand his being out there. He just sits on his bed and . . ."

"And what?" Averil has a smile on his lips, his face and hand following her voice in their own bedroom to the windows, back to the rocker.

"And he listens."

"You read well. You have a lovely voice for reading, and I'm sure he only wants to hear." He crosses his long legs on the bed, fluffs the feather pillows behind him, rubs his temples with his slender fingers. The only part of him he cannot maneuver to his liking is his hair, which triumphs wildly on his head, thick and brown, a few gray strands rising even more mutinously above the rest, coarse and cantankerous. He has the ruffled yet refined look of an eccentric scholar, a chess player in the park, a musician.

"He annoys me," Julia says. She adjusts her magnifying eyeglasses and returns to *Jude the Obscure,* but it is not the same as before. She is self-conscious. While she reads, she begins wondering what the man heard, if he heard her voice take on the personalities of Jude and Arabella, if he heard them slaughter their pig. Now her voice is lower, her chair closer to Averil, her fingers flipping through on their own to find the end of the chapter.

After *Jude,* she reads him some short stories. He doesn't like them as well; they end too quickly, he says. He likes to go on and on. He loved *Anna Karenina.* He never wanted the party to end. But Julia enjoys the short stories and the poems. She can read them twice in one evening if she wants. If they were powerful, she can recast their spell easily. And Averil does have his own books. It isn't as if he must depend completely on her.

The man across the way, however, is still a problem.

She and Averil moved in only a month ago. From Kansas. Julia's new Chicago job, a surprise transfer, paid so much more they couldn't afford not to move. They'd always been strapped for money. For a while, Averil had had to sell cosmetics over the phone. No amount of love for their house in the country could compete with the money she would make. Their move was simple; they hired a van line, had the condominium painted, the floors sanded, the locks changed, before they ever arrived. Julia had only to stand in the hallway and direct the men. "In the study . . . ," she would say, "in the bedroom, . . . down in storage," and their furniture glided into new places, filling available space. She led Averil through the rooms. His hands, clumsy and out of sync with his body in the new rooms, sought the familiar objects of their lives: the smooth round oak table he'd sanded himself, a cold marble vanity stand, the hairy surface of his recliner where his cat Sophie slept, was now sleeping.

It took him no time at all to adjust to the layout. The noise was different. Sirens still startle him in the night. Helicopters and human voices can make him clutch Julia, whose heart leaps for him. It is only then, blackness surrounding both of them, together in a shared blindness, that she mistrusts their judgment. Moving was not good, she thinks. We have done the wrong thing. In these moments she feels anything could happen, that she has so little control in the world that nothing, no place, is safe.

But Averil relaxes, slips into sleep trustingly. His breath against her throat is sweet, not like an adult's but like a child's, clear. His faith in her can calm her; if he trusts her, she must be trustworthy.

Of course, when fall and winter come the windows will be closed. The storm windows will be on, the new drapes hung to insulate even further. It isn't as if they couldn't, even now, close up the windows. They can afford air conditioning. They can afford thin metal blinds that allow light without eyes. But Julia loves air, fresh air. She loves sunlight, even cloudlight, cool and wet. Perhaps because she has lived with Averil for so long, she doesn't bother with much electric lighting. She reads by a soft bulb at night. The rest of the apartment is dark. Light from the window means, for Averil, weather, elements, heat, gradation. It seems unfair to deny him those, to bathe him in the mute hues of electricity and civilization. And so Julia refuses to bow to the man in the window. He doesn't bother Averil; of course, Averil can't see him as he sits on the bed, head turned, listening. His room is dark but a light from the hall cuts an angle of pale yellow that shows him in shadow. He is black, muscular, listening.

Averil has never seen. Anything. Julia still cannot, after ten years of trying, imagine such a world. The great unfairness is that he would be so good a looker at things, so attentive, given the chance. She sometimes strikes deals with whatever God exists: give him sight and I'll give up my feet (my hands, my voice, ten years of my life). Give him sight for a day and I'll give up all our money. Give him sight and I'll give him up.

But what a shock it would be, at forty-four, to suddenly be endowed with a new sense. It would not be the same as taking one away, which is all Julia can think to compare it to. It might be as if she one day woke up clairvoyant, possessing the sixth sense. But if that were so, everyone she knew or met would be tragic, their lives spilled open before her. A mixed blessing.

Sophie cat escapes one day while Julia is working. Averil, when he phones her, can hardly speak. She hears him bang his palm on the table. "I've called her and called her, but she doesn't know where she is." His voice sounds as if someone is choking him, forcing him to speak.

"Was it the back door or the front, Ave? Is she in the building or not?"

For a moment he says nothing. Surely he can remember that? For what must be the millionth time, Julia tries to put herself in his mind; how does the world right itself once it has been jumbled? Is it lining up, like numbers? Is it returning to mass, like mercury?

"The back. She's outside, of course. Would I be this upset if she were still in the building?" He then hangs up on his wife.

When Julia arrives home minutes later (she is amazed at how easy it is to leave work—no one to answer to), Sophie is sunning on the rear brick wall of the building, her tummy exposed, back rubbing against the stone. Julia grabs her so tightly the cat lets out a small breathless squeal. She fights valiantly but Julia's anger is bigger, stronger. They both cease when they hear Averil, standing at the door, at the top of the second flight of stairs. "Kitty, kitty, Sophie, Sophie," he says in a voice that doesn't care who is listening.

Julia drops Sophie to the ground not fifty yards from her husband and backs up. Sophie runs without hesitating between his legs, into the kitchen. Averil pauses a moment, still holding the door with one hand, his free hand in the air, as if he's heard Julia. He cocks his head, then slowly shuts the screen door. "Sophie," Julia hears him say. "Come here, old girl." The other, heavy inner door shuts, leaving her alone. She watches Averil through the window, which is so high she can see only the top of the refrigerator opening and closing. Sophie will get a treat.

When Julia turns, her heart calming, tears of relief forming in her eyes, she faces the man from the window, coming up the steps.

"Excuse me," he says, and her heart immediately stutters back to life, her tears disappear. He keeps his deep cow-brown eyes on hers, his gym bag held away from himself to navigate around her. He passes, jogging to his back steps, skipping every other one on his way up.

Milton is off limits. Not by Averil's insistence, but his wife's. She cannot shake the poem that leaves the poet dreaming of the sight of his own wife in his blindness, waking to darkness, to the interminable nightmare.

"It's powerful for everyone, Jule," Averil will tell her, annoyed. "You haven't cornered the market on responding to it, you know." But even *Paradise Lost* leaves her unsettled, though Averil loves Satan's logic.

At home, Averil makes friends with the retired cop upstairs. They share a love of railroads; the man has a set replicating the Southern Pacific line running through his apartment, a computer terminal to regulate bridge droppings, grain loadings, rail changes. Averil now sometimes wakes at night laughing, hearing the squeaky hoot of a tiny engine through their bedroom ceiling.

Julia heats with protective love for Averil when she thinks of him trying to explain his own love of trains to the cop. She can only imagine it; she would never ask, "How did you tell him you love the motion, the thrumming through your body as the train picks up speed, the snaking out into the landscape?"

"Right," the cop in her mind answers, smiling behind his hand. But of course that isn't the way it is; nothing is ever rendered quite itself in speculation. Averil's cop perhaps nods emphatically, saying he knows precisely how Averil feels, the lulling of the wheels, groove to groove with rail, the homey enclosure of one car, then the next, the crossing between them, suspended between warm worlds, each smelling peculiarly of train, of trainness—leather, smoke, oil, wool, men traveling.

Averil and the cop, Frank, ride the El into the city often, sometimes simply riding the Loop route and coming back without getting off. Friday's Express conductor knows them. The cop tells stories from his years on the force. They ride once into the Southside and Averil can tell the difference when the doors slide open, the new tension, the cooking odors that float in at every platform. Donuts, Thai food, pizza, popcorn. His coat and hair, when he returns, have collected the city's odors the way they used to collect the country's, woodsmoke and snow.

"Are you happy here?" she asks him over dinner.

"I'm surprised to say that I am," he tells her, sipping his wine carefully. He collects wine, attends tasting events at a liquor store a few blocks away. Behind him on the counter is a beautiful rack of bottles, their colors pale and floral in the room.

"You ask as if you aren't happy here yourself," he says to her. "Are you?"

"Your bottles are very pretty in this light," she says, momentarily satisfied with the room, their new life. "I guess I'm happy. I miss our yard."

"I miss the land, too. I miss exploring without worrying about getting lost. But I'm getting better. I feel comfortable in this neighborhood and downtown. It's good to have the library near."

"I think you could be happy anywhere."

He pauses a long moment. "That's possible."

Strangely, it bothers her to know he is adjusting to the city, to know that when he wakes in the night he now laughs instead of grabbing her in terror, to know that he depends on her less. She wonders at her motives in marrying Averil. Did she really want a child instead? A man unlike other men, one who followed her lead without having a real choice? Before Averil, her relationships with men ended just at the point she felt herself losing control. Or, to be more exact, at the point when the men no longer relinquished control. They would withdraw, always assuming Julia would follow, concede, thereby balancing the power. Both parties would have leverage, these men seemed to argue. But Julia would surprise them by also withdrawing. Permanently.

Yet she did not seek out passive men. In fact, it was Averil's argumentativeness that first attracted her. She'd signed up for a classics seminar at the University of Kansas one fall more than eleven years ago, and Averil had been the most vocal student there, arguing incessantly over interpretations and critics. Eventually the professor, a stunningly sexy young woman, had had to ask him after class to quit interrupting and allow her to teach. "If you could see her," Julia said to him then, walking him to the campus bus that night, "you wouldn't be able to disagree with her."

"So you're saying sight's a hindrance, in reality?" He'd laughed, smoothing his face with his broad hand as if to control more laughter. Later, Julia discovered it was a gesture to ensure there wasn't food left on his chin or mustache. "Or are you saying that most men are led by their genitals and not their heads?" he said. "I hadn't thought of what an advantage I must have. But where are the hordes?" He'd spread his arms, white cane bouncing in the air. "There must be hundreds of liberated women waiting for such a man." The campus was empty, a strong fall wind swaying the trees. His hair, in the streetlight, mussed itself into a variety of patterns. He seemed to be looking just above the campanile on the next rise, just at the point where a fat, almost perfect harvest moon rose. Julia loved him then, suddenly and without hesitation.

When his bus pulled up, moments later, he boarded still smiling, and when he sat down he waved directly at Julia, confident she was still there watching him.

"I wouldn't be happy without you," he says, much later, from nowhere. "Perhaps that's obvious, but I wouldn't be here at all without you, let alone happy."

She doesn't respond, at least not in a way he can sense.

"Julia? Come here, please." His hands, both warm from his cup of hot tea, caress her face. "Sweet Julia," he murmurs, his thumbs pressed expertly underneath her eyes, smoothing the soft spots so that she won't cry.

She forgets about the man across the ten-foot space between the buildings after winter sets in. The cold arrives in a
night; trees dump all their leaves in a single afternoon. Storm
windows seal their apartment like a lid seals a jar. Occasionally, on rare sunny days, Julia snaps their bedroom blinds
open. Always surprised by the proximity of the windows
across from theirs, she stares into the space between. Brown
bricks like prison walls. Upstairs, porcelain cats line the sills.
Extravagant silk flowers in another window. She cannot explain the feeling she has seeing these things. Why not a real
cat? Why not live flowers? The windows do not seem like
those of living, breathing people, but windows for her own
observation alone, scenic, art. Leaning close to the glass she
can make out a gray strip of cloud above. Where does it end?
Where does it begin? Weather here is not predictable, does not
creep or slide across an enormous sky. Here, it is stark, imme-
diate, surprising.

One of Averil's favorite pastimes in Kansas was predicting
the weather. He knew when he woke what sort of day it would
be—if his head hurt, there would be rain or snow before night.
Or if there were a certain yellow smell in the air, a quality of
the wind, he would know tornadoes were due. When he heard
cicadas, drunk even at sunrise on the sound of their own
noise, the day would be a still scorcher. The first day of spring
or fall was never on its prescribed day, but always on the day
when the wind shifted, took a hard turn; he explained to Julia
that the birds used the high winds to travel north or south.
Their coming and going was what really divided the seasons.

Across from her a shade snaps up. A black hand steadies it,
pulls it down, tugging to line it up. Julia, in remembering her
old home, standing at the windows there and watching the
sky, is shocked motionless by the extraordinary contrast the
window across from her makes. The second shade comes up,

is steadied, evened, a third. Julia lowers herself to the floor, eyes at the sill, watching. She sees a bed, a white chenille spread like the one she had when she was young, a rounded dresser, its wood drawers scalloped, a rocking chair, something—a poster, a painting, a flag—hanging on the far wall, bright colors against plain white. The room is precisely like her own in its floor plan, a mirror image, the door on her right mimicked by another door there. Both are open halfway. The man, after a brief glance in his dresser mirror—he squats leaning back, touches his short hair in little pats—steps through the half-open door into his hallway. Julia sees him without seeing him. He now goes to his kitchen, perhaps turns on the faucet, rinses a sponge, switches on a radio, peels an orange, sits at the table and reads his mail.

She opens her eyes. Four-thirty and the light has disappeared, the sun has already sunk behind some tall building to the west of her.

She knows Averil has noticed that the shades now are up almost all the time; he feels cool air radiate from the windows. He doesn't ask her but sometimes stands before them, tracing the colder air with his palms, squares of glass. Though it annoys her that his tact won't allow him to question her, she doesn't know how she would explain. She feels as if they are waiting for something, as if opening the shades will encourage its arrival. What is it? she wonders, lying on their bed, running her eyes again and again over the porcelain cats, the fake flowers.

Julia has had little practice observing other lives, spying, as it were. It surprises her to hear arguments from the apartment below, doors slamming and plaster trickling. When she retrieves her mail, other tenants' magazines must be sifted through to find her own. What curious tastes they have: the faceless woman next door who receives endless catalogs for underwear and sex toys; baby magazines come for the fighting couple; and body-building ones for Frank, the retired cop. She meets them in the laundry room, dragging their dirty sheets from basket to washer to dryer, or in the parking lot when she and Averil go for a drive. They say hello and Averil answers, smiling, but Julia only nods, not quite meeting their eyes. Sometimes at night she looks at their lighted windows and tries to imagine their lives (stacked, she thinks of them, one on top of the other) from the brief bits of them she catches—a family around a table playing cards, a naked pregnant woman, standing in the light of an open refrigerator drinking from a milk carton.

The man (her man, she thinks, as if even fleeting familiarity with his habits made him known to her) directly across from their apartment is rarely home, or, at least, rarely in his bedroom. No one else is ever there. The bed does not go unmade. His shades are at half-mast except at night, when they are drawn and he is the bulky shadow that crosses them now and then.

When Julia lived in the country, fifteen minutes from Lawrence and the university, forty-five from Kansas City, it occurred to her only occasionally that she had no close friends. Her life with Averil, so far from great numbers of people, seemed naturally and comfortably isolated. The people they saw regularly—the Eudora rural postman, their neighbors whose cows sometimes found their way into Averil's cucumbers and tomatoes, Julia's officemates—were touchstones, places where an independent life met with a public one. But in a place as public as a city a lone soul stood out—not literally, for it was easy to be alone—but figuratively. Why, in a city of millions, Julia wondered, would one choose to be alone? Even Averil, the epitome of self-sufficiency, had Frank upstairs.

Julia sits at her desk, staring at the blinking orange cursor on her computer terminal. *Who?* she types, then leans on the o and fills a few lines. *Robin?* she writes. On the other side of a transparent screen sits her secretary, listening to a terrible lunch hour radio show that Julia has made her turn off more than once. Robin is in her early thirties, a chatterer who likes to laugh. She's recently divorced, probably a little lonely herself, but something keeps Julia and her at a distance. It could be as simple as their relationship—employee and employer— but Julia doesn't think so. Robin has the kind of self-confidence that Julia is made shy by. When Julia interviewed her, Robin asked most of the questions. Why had Julia left Kansas? What did her husband do? Did she have children? This question wasn't meant unkindly, but it stung Julia nonetheless. She hadn't had to answer it for a few years, and her stock response was rusty.

"My husband and I have always been happy as a family of two," she told Robin, stiffening. But Robin wasn't willing, as most people were, to take the hint and back off.

"But husband and wife don't count as family," she'd said, practically pleading with her big blue eyes. "I mean, family means children. Don't get me wrong—I understand. My husband and I just got divorced because I wanted kids and my husband, ex-husband, thought like you. He thought the two of us were plenty." She'd laughed good-naturedly, and Julia had decided to hire her. Now, looking back, it was as if she had tried to introduce some new sensibility into her daily routine. With Robin only a partition away, perhaps a new outlook would rub off.

Robin gives advice easily, confidently, though Julia rarely takes advantage of it. Robin is quick to compliment clothing and hairstyles, quick to condemn certain members of the art department downstairs, the editors upstairs. She is sharp, and only rarely does Julia disagree with her evaluations. Which is why she is both tempted to and fearful of asking what Robin thinks. How painful would it be to be under her critical eye? Is that what intimacy is, exposure of soft spots? Julia cannot picture a time when it would be possible for her to confess her doubts about her marriage. I'd like to know, she thinks. Did I marry Averil because he was blind or in spite of it? Neither, she answers herself.

Julia watches Robin through the partition between them. Robin smiles at something one of the morons on the noon-time radio show says. Julia thinks that if Robin herself were worried, she would phone one of those radio talk shows and ask the host. They might have a long talk about it. *You married him because you loved him,* the host would say, and of course that was the truth. But why did she love Averil? Julia wonders. And where had that love come from?

My husband is blind, Julia remembers telling Robin, later in the interview. In most cases that successfully closed a conversation, answered any number of questions about other issues (Why don't you have children? My husband is blind. What does he do for a living? Well, he stays at home. He's blind, you see.), but Robin's face stayed open, curious. *Yes,* she seemed to say, *and what else?*

In February, Averil signs up for a cooking class at a French restaurant two blocks from their building. Pastries and sweets are emphasized. He's always done most of the cooking because Julia can't seem to ever taste anything she's made. If she wants to know how a recipe turned out, she has to save part of it for the next day, then reheat it and see. Her taste buds, after hours of testing, fade away. Averil loves to cook. He has an extensive library of cassette tapes, all of Julia reading recipes. Because he always goes overboard on spices, Julia leaves him reminders in the middle of the ingredients ("Remember how far you can stretch a pinch of red pepper, Ave," or, "Contrary to popular belief, garlic does not make the world go round").

But French sweets are a luxury. When she gets home from work, there will be butter and sugar in the air, custards and vanilla. His teacher's voice on the tape, among the noise of aluminum utensils, instructing on folding eggs and loading an icing tube. Averil will hurry through dinner—hamburgers or casseroles, since he has spent most of the day on dessert— and then produce Coeur à la Crème, éclairs, Coffee Torte, or, the teacher's specialty, Chocolate Bag, a dark chocolate container filled with white chocolate mousse, fresh fruits, whipped cream. Averil brings it to the table, the thumb of each hand having measured the amount of raspberry glaze on the plate.

"These are beautiful," Julia says. She likes knowing his fingers have been everywhere in the dessert, feeling for fullness and fluff. "Do you badger this teacher like you did our professor?"

He sits and smiles at her, apron still around his sweatsuit. "She's European. They know how to take a badgering. Plus, I've got the whole class on tape. I don't think I could stand to hear myself yammering away."

"This is delicious."

"Isn't it? I thought I would take Frank one upstairs. The recipe makes four, and they don't keep."

"What about the other?"

He shrugs. Julia feels a wave of self-pity flow through her: they know no one to take a dessert to. For some reason she thinks of the man in the windows for a second. Of course, that is absurd. Then she thinks of Robin.

When she calls, Robin has just gotten out of the bathtub.

Her hair is wet and she hasn't eaten dinner, which Julia assumes will be a polite way of declining the invitation, but Robin says she will be there as soon as she can. Julia instantly checks the wall clock. In just four hours, she thinks, she will be safely in bed, alone with Averil. The evening will be over.

Robin sits in Sophie's hairy chair, though Averil thought to warn her beforehand. The two of them laugh when the cat begins complaining. Julia makes coffee in the kitchen, listening to the sputter of the maker, wiping down the counter, throwing crumbs away, rinsing out and drying the coffee cups. When the machine spits the last of the water through, Julia takes a big breath and brings in the tray.

Averil sits leaning forward on the couch, facing Robin. "She's adjusted remarkably to the move," he is saying, and for a split second Julia thinks he means her—but he would be lying, for she hasn't adjusted at all—then realizes with relief they still are talking about Sophie, who circles Robin's feet. Julia gives Averil the same objective critical appraisal she gave the living room before Robin came over, wishing she could straighten and plump him up, the way she had the couch cushions. He is thin and mussed. He'd changed from his cooking sweatsuit into corduroys and a green cotton sweater, which emphasizes the color of his eyes, but his hair, as always, flops and sprouts everywhere. Julia smoothes it when she sits down next to him.

"I like to see people's homes," Robin says, to both of them, looking around the room. "You get a better sense of someone, seeing their places. When I think of you now, at home, I'll think of Sophie here, and Averil." Robin blinks over her coffee. "Averil was telling me about a famous chocolate sack."

"Good grief, I'd forgotten the Chocolate Bag," Averil says. He stands abruptly, hitting his knee on the coffee table and jiggling the cups. "Give me a minute to set the glaze." He walks deliberately to the kitchen, hands on either side of him. It's as if he hasn't lived here for nine months now, or as if Julia had moved the furniture without telling him.

When she looks back at Robin, Julia would like to explain, tell her that her visit is making Averil nervous, that usually he navigates the house as well as Sophie or herself.

"When I was condominium hunting," Robin says, "I visited probably a hundred places. I drove my realtor crazy, but I just love looking at other people's apartments. It's so much better than visiting the vacant ones. I think that must be a real estate trick—make the place look lived in."

Julia nods. She could confide now, if she wanted, that she enjoys looking in her neighbors' windows. It was sort of the same thing, wasn't it? Surely she could find a way to phrase it that would make it sound comic, sociable. But there is a crash in the kitchen. She is at the door before she knows she's moved. Averil stands at the counter hurriedly feeling around him. A broken plate is on the floor. "Ave?" she says, quietly.

"Dropped my bag," he says. "How bad is it?"

On the floor the chocolate casing has broken into several corners of its former delicate sack-self.

"Can we save it?" he asks, a smile in his voice.

It is ruined, of course. Julia kneels before him and begins picking up pieces. "Go on out," she hisses. "I'll finish this. Go talk with her."

Averil doesn't move. His hands are limp at his sides.

"Go on," Julia says, angrier than she realized she was. "You won't step on anything, just go. She's waiting."

He leaves awkwardly and she finishes picking up the pieces. She arranges them on another dessert plate, topping them with the mousse and fresh berries, dolloping whipped cream. She sets it on the counter and assesses her work. It looks good enough to have been intentionally in pieces. Chocolate Corners, she could name it. The glaze forms a sheet of red in the base of the plate, dotted with tiny seeds.

Averil's anger smolders, simmers like coals until Robin has gone home. He then hardens his face at Julia, directly at her, and tells her he is furious.

"About what?" she says, slipping away from his eyes, loading the tray, and carrying it into the kitchen. "Robin's plate is completely empty. She loved it," she calls.

"Come here."

"What?" she runs the disposer to give herself time. She is afraid of him, ashamed of herself, ready to rewind the last months of their lives and start anew. *I want my old life*, she bargains. Not even a real trade, just getting back what was once hers.

Averil stands at the doorway. "Turn that off." She switches the disposal off, its blades grinding one final time. "I won't be treated like a child, Julia."

They have fought so rarely that it takes Julia a moment to recognize that this could be one. Or it could be an admission of wrongdoing on her part. For a moment the possibilities are before her; it all depends on how she responds, but she feels nearly blank. It frightens her to realize that if their lives could be rewound she would most likely repeat the scene they have just gone through. And that makes an apology a lie.

"Robin liked you," she chooses to say.

"Glad to have met your standards," he says. "Glad to have passed the test, despite my shameful showing in . . ." He's too angry to continue. His hands, the hands she loves more than anything in the world, clench at his hips.

"Don't be angry with me," she says, tears filling the space behind her eyes and nose. She is pleading, and though she knows it is manipulative, it is also true. "I can't stand to have you angry with me."

Very solidly he hits the two sides of the doorframe with his fists. Julia wishes she could see the life they'd be leading in another nine months. The past or the future—she'd take either one.

Before the rail prices go up for spring, Averil makes a trip with Frank to Canada on the train. Julia is careful at the station with them. She would like to tell Averil to call her every night, but doesn't know whether it is a request a wife would make of a seeing husband, and therefore doesn't ask.

That night she cannot go to sleep in their bedroom. She hears people on the back steps, creaking in Frank's apartment, slamming and crashing everywhere. Taking Sophie with her, she checks both doors yet another time, then looks in closets, latches the windows. Finally she settles on the loveseat in the study because its door has a lock.

The second night is no better, though she has primed herself all day for a night alone. Because she didn't sleep well the night before, she turns in early, watching TV. She plans to fall asleep with it on, letting it lull her through the night. But by two she knows it will not work. She keeps turning the sound down to listen for other noises. Then she and Sophie are back at the doors, closets, windows, eventually asleep together, fitfully, on the loveseat in the study.

On day three she calls work and takes a personal day.

"You all right?" Robin asks, concerned.

"Fine, really," Julia says. Robin has taken to asking about Averil and the cat. She's grown fonder of Julia through them, though no closer. "I'm tired," Julia admits. "I haven't been able to sleep since Averil left." It is a huge confession for her and she feels herself blushing.

"Oh, I know how that is," Robin says. "Would you like company? I'd be glad to come by."

Julia thanks her but declines. The confession was enough for one day.

With the day free, she decides to spring-clean. Dust and cat hair have been settling for months on the curtains and throw rugs. She exhausts herself, finishing one room and then immediately starting another. After she takes two last loads of wash to the laundry room, she lies on her bed for a rest, happy on the clean comforter.

When she wakes, the room is dark. What's wakened her is thunder. The windows shake and she looks out, half expecting to see trees and clouds; the brick wall seems an affront, there to startle her. She goes through the apartment snapping on all the lights, admiring the cleanliness, the fresh way everything smells. It is only after she's sat down with a bowl of chicken soup that she remembers she has wet laundry in the washers.

Chicago reflects against the clouds, a clay-pot orange. For a moment Julia stands outside her door wondering how she ever got here. She is not the person she'd imagined growing into; this is not the life she'd seen. She knows these two things without being able to name what she *had* imagined. Two quarters in her palm, an umbrella in the other hand, she makes a run for the laundry room.

He is there. Like the brick wall, he seems to have leaped into existence at the precise moment she looks up. He takes her breath away. Expecting the worst for three days still has not prepared her for his presence.

"Oh," she manages.

"Hello," he says.

She focuses on her washers, which are against the near wall. Without thinking, she stuffs both loads into one dryer, inserts her quarters quickly, and slams the door, sure that he is watching.

"Hey," he says, as she heads, chin down, to the door. She looks up. "You lost something." For a moment she does not connect his gesture with his words. *Yes, exactly, I've lost a great deal*, she thinks. He points; she continues staring at his face. "There," he says, his voice irritated. Finally Julia looks at the floor. One of Averil's socks.

"Don't look at me like you're my next victim, lady. Go on now, go on. Let me be." He nudges his head forward in the direction in which he wishes her to disappear. His forehead is wrinkled in anger or confusion or both. Frustration, Julia sees. She backs away, leaving the sock in the middle of the yellow floor.

It is only when she is at the door, almost safely on her return trip, that she notices he is folding clothing. Not only is he folding clothing, it is children's clothing: tiny shorts, tiny shirts, flowered panties, red overalls with blue sailboats, green turtleneck with white hearts, bright yellow socks with the smallest ducks swimming round and round on them. And standing behind him, thumb in mouth, is a small boy. "Daddy?" the boy says. "Who's that lady?"

When Averil returns, they are newly tender with one another. He had a wonderful time, despite missing her. He and Frank will make it an annual trip. Julia holds him very close and replenishes her supply of him. She does not confess her weakness without him. It is only then that she understands he lied before when he said he wouldn't be happy without her. Not that he would wish her gone, just that he is a survivor, while she is not. She married him because she needed him, still needs him.

Sophie cat wakes them both one night, clucking her open mouth at the window, illuminated by the outdoor lights. Averil sits up and listens. He puts his hand solidly on Julia's arm, just above the elbow. "Hear them?" he whispers.

Hear who? Julia scans the room, hears only her heart in her head. The shapes of their furniture in this arrangement is familiar now, and she runs her eyes over it for reassurance. Who? She can make out no noise outside herself other than the cat, whose shadow against the wall shows her open mouth and tongue, clucking.

"Listen," Averil says, still gripping her arm. "Close your eyes and listen."

Once her eyes are shut her heartbeat dissolves into the oceanic sound of herself, and the room dissolves into a purer darkness. There is only this bed, two naked bodies on it, Averil's hand holding her arm. And above her, above them, shouting down at a light-speckled city, flies a flock of geese on a south wind.

Substitute

Jo Jo Lesher Esquivel shut the sliding glass door between herself and her six-year-old son Tommy, who wailed himself purple-faced on the other side. As the door closed he was rendered silent; the glass was quite thick for that of a hotel, and the outside air had a certain dense murkiness to it that muffled sound. Jo Jo could hear herself breathing. She felt ten pounds heavier simply due to humidity.

She already regretted having brought Tommy to Atlanta. He had hated the plane because his ears plugged and he'd spent the trip from Memphis yawning, popping his jaw, and requesting chewing gum from a thoroughly too-kind stewardess. Jo Jo would have left him at home with his father, but she and Manny fought before she left and, for some reason that now escaped her, part of her victory in the argument included taking Tommy to Atlanta.

Her housemate from graduate school was getting married at last. Jo Jo, thirty-six years old, was maid of honor, a role she found amusing as well as embarrassing. Della had called early in the summer, in love with one of her students, nine years her junior. He played classical violin, but also bluegrass fiddle. He studied engineering, but also built plastic rockets. But also. He was perfect. Jo Jo snorted to think of all Della's other perfect men—though this one was hanging on, his greatest virtue. "Just think of this," Della had concluded on the telephone, soberly, "I'm thirty-four years old, more likely to be

shot by terrorists than married, and here's a guy who's gaga.
How do I know another man will ever want to make love with
me again?"

"I hate you!" Tommy screamed from inside, loud enough to
penetrate the glass. His face paled when he saw his mother, in
a flash, emerge from reverie and yank the door open. She
grabbed him by the flimsy lapels of his traveling clothes before he could duck.

"You never ever say that." Her voice was amazingly calm,
given her fierce eyes. "It's a rule. Understand?"

He said nothing, which Jo Jo correctly interpreted as acqui-
escence.

"Let's go find the bride," she said cheerfully, straightening
his collar and swatting him playfully on the behind.

Della's family had overrun the hotel swimming pool. They
were, one and all, towheaded and fair-skinned, white as al-
binos; even those only related by marriage resembled blood
kin. For the first twenty minutes Jo Jo and Tommy sat survey-
ing the scene from under an umbrella. Tommy had picked up
his mother's habit of looking before he leaped—and, like her,
not out of caution so much as criticism. Jo Jo was uncomfort-
able with his imitation; she felt as if the two of them were a
couple of predator cats stalking a group of dopey fawns.

"Don't get in over your head," she told Tommy when he
finally rose. He brushed her off with the back of his hand. Jo Jo
pulled a pack of cigarettes from her heap of swimming para-
phernalia. She always smoked when she and Manny fought;
he considered it unfeminine and she found it distracting.

Della came dripping out of the pool. "You made such a
quiet entrance I missed it altogether." She shook her frizzy
white hair down on Jo Jo.

"We came in the back door. I wore shades." Though Jo Jo resisted, Della gave her an awkward hug around the neck.

"Where's Manny?"

"Home stewing."

"Oh . . ." Della's face fell. Conflict always disappointed her.

"Your brother here?" Jo Jo asked.

"Both of them. There's Michael with his kids . . ."

"No, the unmarried one."

Della frowned.

"I'm joking," Jo Jo said. "Only joking. Manny and I are swell. Two peas in a pudding. Happy as hermit crabs."

Della looked worriedly down at her.

"Sit," Jo Jo commanded.

Della pulled up Tommy's chair and fell into it.

"Besides, your brother and I wouldn't last. I don't have even one freckle."

Della snickered. "See my sister?" she said.

Jo Jo watched as Patsy wound a towel around her waist and flung her long light hair behind her shoulder. She went to another table without looking at them. "Check."

"She's quite angry."

"Why's that?" Jo Jo asked.

"I hurt her feelings when I made you matron of honor."

"Matron?"

"Well, sure, cause you're married."

"Make her matron of honor, I don't care."

"She'd be a maid. Besides," Della said, "I don't want to. Where has she been when the shit's hit the fan in my life?"

Jo Jo looked over Della's shoulder for Tommy. Already he'd made himself leader of the kids, shouting "Marco" while they responded "Polo."

"I'll tell you where she's been," Della continued. "Not available. No comment. That's where."

Jo Jo watched her son cheating, squinting his eyes, and pretending to flail while making a beeline for Della's smallest nephew. With his dark tan and near-black hair, Tommy looked exotic and misplaced in their midst, like a foreign coin in a handful of nickels.

"Tommy's so brown," Della said, following Jo Jo's eyes.

"It's that hot Latino blood of his father's," Jo Jo said. "Nice suit you have there."

"You like it?" Della looked down over her torso.

Jo Jo forced herself to give her friend a good appraisal, chest and all. Della had had a mastectomy eight years ago, while they were living together. Jo Jo could not discern a difference between her friend's two breasts; in fact, she couldn't remember which one was missing. "Very nice," she said, abruptly looking back toward the children, as if one of them had called her name.

Della leaned toward her over the table and in a stage whisper said, "It's a waterproof suction cup." She sat back, thumping her simulated breast. "You really ought not to smoke. Especially since I can't anymore."

Jo Jo flipped her burning cigarette into a puddle. "My dress is a joke," she said. "My mother's spastic maid sewed it."

"Really? Patsy's and Ellen's are very nice." Della began to describe the dresses for her. They sounded nothing like her own. There were to be baskets of flowers, straw hats. Jo Jo got a special bouquet in her basket. "Now why is your dress so bad?" Della asked at last, tilting her head earnestly and twiddling an earring.

"It looks like I made it myself. I hope that basket is a big old thing."

"Well," Della said, concerned, "maybe the dress could be altered . . ."

"Just joking," Jo Jo said. "So where's the blushing groom?

I already recognized your whole family and he's not out here."

"Are you sure your dress is okay?"

"Positive. I'll do you proud, don't fret. Where is he?"

"Well, he's inside organizing. He's leading a tour of the Maitland campus at three. He doesn't know how my family will hate it, poor Stu. They're going to take one look at his un-air-conditioned station wagon and his itinerary and hightail it back to the pool. Of course, you are invited as well, but I already told him we had to go shopping."

"We do?"

"Something borrowed, something blue. Something on sale, something brand spanking new. Oh, Jo Jo . . ." Della was suddenly taken with a fit of affection and reached across to hold Jo Jo's hand before Jo Jo could escape it. "I'm very glad you're here. I know you're going to think Stu's a nerd, but I'm glad you're here anyway."

Della had truly terrible taste in men. The last one Jo Jo had known well was during graduate school in Chicago. Stevie. Also white-haired and freckled, but brawny in a sort of Nordic way that was unlike the rest of Della's family. He'd hated Della's many cats and had been the one, finally, who forced her to go to her gynecologist about the lump in her breast. "By the way," he'd said on his way out for the last time, "you also have a yeast infection." Even in memory, Jo Jo felt compelled to flip him off.

Jo Jo had been privy to many of Della's lousy relationships. She'd lived upstairs, where the hall bathroom was over Della's bedroom downstairs. Jo Jo, who often sat brooding in the bath, heard Della and her boyfriends. Della would one minute be yelling about her need to be alone to finish her dissertation, the next crying for whoever it was to please stay, please spend the night. Jo Jo, whose man problems seemed always to involve turning down marriage proposals, could not make sense of Della. Many a time she'd advised forgetting him, whoever he was. Many a time Della had stared back uncomprehending. But when push finally came to shove, it was the men who went. Della had always put her professional life first—doctorate, grants, job, tenure—while boyfriends and other friends followed behind, important, but only as comic relief from her academic work. Jo Jo figured that Della's decision to marry now had everything to do with having gotten tenure the year before.

"You get a big raise?" she asked as they pawed through racks of dresses at T. J. Maxx.

"Seventeen percent," Della said, absently. "Stu figured it out. You like this?" She held up a dress with hoops.

Jo Jo raised an eyebrow. "If I wanted to wear wires, I'd put on a hanger," she said.

Della laughed too hard. It was something Jo Jo had forgotten about her friend until just then—she thought Jo Jo was too funny. Jo Jo moved a few steps down.

"You always could make me laugh," Della said when she'd recovered. "Remember at the hospital? You came and made me laugh every day."

Jo Jo continued thumbing through the size eight rack, but she wasn't paying any attention to what her fingers were doing. She was trying to picture the hospital. All that came to mind was its facade, which Jo Jo had driven by daily for years on her way to school. Except for the morning she'd taken Della there for the initial biopsy, she didn't have a single image of the place—not Della's room, not her doctor. What jokes? She recalled sitting in a coffee shop waiting for time to pass, to learn whether it was malignant or benign. Malevolent or benevolent? she remembered thinking. She narrowed her eyes at Della now, trying to see her in a hospital bed, but nothing came. That time seemed to have left her completely.

Later, at lunch in Atlanta's artsy-craftsy mall, Jo Jo tried to work the conversation back around to the hospital. She hated to have things unclear. But Della was engrossed with wedding and Jo Jo reluctantly let it slide.

"Stu's mother made us choose a silver pattern. I mean, Jo Jo, I already have silver, for one thing, and for another, we aren't really starting a household or anything. I *have* a household. I've had it for quite a while. I don't want any more silver." She picked up an asparagus spear with her fingers and put it on her fork. "Though it *is* a pretty pattern. His mother also *made* us get separate hotel rooms. I felt like such a fool checking in, but she wants to act like this is some normal wedding, like we're both twenty-three-year-old virgins or some damn thing."

"So," Jo Jo said, "I think you should describe for this woman her son in bed."

Della laughed too hard again. She lifted her Bibb lettuce in search of more olives. "You know, he *was* a virgin," she said, blushing. "I couldn't remember the last time I'd encountered such a thing. Can you?"

Jo Jo shook her head. "It's sort of an endearing problem, though."

"Anyway, his mother couldn't believe I was never in a sorority. When she found out how old I was, I could practically see her brain working, subtracting Stu's age from mine, then my age from hers. I wanted to yell out, 'Yes, I'm closer to your age than his, I confess.'"

"But you didn't."

"No, I didn't. Inside, I'm as clever as you, but outside I'm a coward." She smiled. "Would you want to know if you had spinach between your front teeth?"

"Sure," Jo Jo said, snapping her mouth shut and running her tongue around her teeth.

Della smiled. "That's *my* kind of joke."

In Della's Volvo, on their way back to the hotel, Della asked the question Jo Jo had been dreading.

"He seems nice," Jo Jo heard herself answering. She and Stu had shaken hands in the lobby; his handshake was of the limp and damp variety. He'd been shepherding people toward his car, but made time to tell Jo Jo how much he'd heard about her. She hated it when people told her how much they'd heard about her. The two of them had taken a sort of mutual dislike to one another immediately, she could tell by the way he'd studied her when he thought she wasn't looking, then smiling phonily when she did look. To him, she must have seemed like trouble. "Now I know what Coke-bottle lenses are all about," she said to Della.

"His vision is something like 20/600. He takes them off for pictures." Della peeked nervously over at Jo Jo. "You'll get used to him. I did. At first he seems really formal and hyper-organized, which he is, but he's other things, too. Although he's an only child, and sometimes they can be a bit spoiled . . ." She trailed off. "You want some iced tea before we go back?"

"Sure."

They drove through at McDonald's, Della wrestling the wheel of the Volvo around the turn. "Two teas," she shouted at the order board.

"Tell them no sugar," Jo Jo said. "This is the South, where the vegetables are overcooked and the iced tea is sweet." She leaned over Della. "No sugar!" she yelled at the board. She sat back. "I hate sugar."

"I don't mind it," Della said, driving to the window.

"'Two tays,'" Jo Jo mimicked as they turned back into traffic. "Lord, some days I really ache for Chicago. Memphis! You wouldn't believe what it's like living in such close proximity to Graceland."

"Stu's family is southern. I find them mostly very sweet. Except his mother, of course. Southerners just seem so friendly. You know, Jo Jo, you even have a little bit of an accent. I know you don't want to, but you do, and I like it. It makes you sound so amiable."

They turned into the hotel parking lot and jolted to a halt in a space. Della switched the engine off and they sat for a moment in the hot sun, the remaining chilliness of air conditioning dying fast around them. Neither of them moved, Jo Jo taking her cue from Della.

"How's Manny?" Della asked, undoing her seat belt and lifting one knee conversationally.

"Ready to return to the pig farm, from whence he came."

"What?"

"Manny's family owns a pig farm in Mexico. I'm ready to deport him. Do you think we could roll down some windows, if we're going to sit out here?"

Della switched the engine on and lowered Jo Jo's window. Jo Jo'd meant to indicate that she was ready to go inside, but Della seemed set on staying in the car.

"I thought he had lots of family money."

"Different family, if you know what I mean."

Della looked perplexed.

"He deals," Jo Jo said, sighing.

"He *deals?*"

"He deals."

"I didn't know he dealt. I thought he just had, you know, *money*, but I didn't know he dealt." Della nodded her head in wonder. "He deals."

"You're saying you didn't know he dealt?"

Della laughed. "Basically," she said.

"We're going to roast like chickens in this auto," Jo Jo said. "C'mon, I'll show you our room. You'll like the art work."

"It'll be just like my room's art work," Della complained, "Parisians on the Champs d' Elysees." But she rolled the windows up and they got out. "Manny deals," she said again as they went through the electric hotel doors. "I can't believe it."

Tommy was in the lobby watching MTV.

"I thought you went touring," Jo Jo said.

"I didn't want to sit on that lady's lap. What's monogamy, Mom?"

"You already asked me that. If you want to see Della giggle, you'll have to come up with a fresh word. Let's go." She held her hand out and he took it.

"Hi, Tommy," Della said.

"Hi, Farmer in the Dell."

"Very funny," Jo Jo said.

"So funny you forgot to laugh," Tommy said for her.

"He has your sense of humor," Della said.

"I resent that," Jo Jo said. "I have a perfectly good sense of humor."

"You're a little devil," Della told Tommy. "Just like your mom."

At their door, Tommy insisted on using the key. His fingers were still chubby from babyhood, dirty in their creases. The rest of him was turning to bone and knob.

"It's upside down," Jo Jo told him.

"I *know* that," he said, reversing the key and exploding into the room.

"Y'all's room is like the Antarctic," Della said.

"Our'all's room is comfortably cool. Would you like a drink? Our'all's bathroom sink is full of ice and beer."

"And Cokes," Tommy said.

"And Cokes," Jo Jo agreed.

"Coke, please," Della said. She sat on Tommy's designated bed. "What lady?"

"What lady what?" Tommy asked.

"What lady whose lap you didn't want to sit on."

"Your husband's mother."

Della nodded. "Did I tell you?" she said knowingly to Jo Jo.

"Your husband reminds me of a giraffe," Tommy told Della.

"Boyfriend," Jo Jo said, bringing in the Cokes.

"Fiancé," Della corrected. "A giraffe?"

"Cause of his neck," Tommy said, stretching his own to demonstrate.

"Yeah? And what do I remind you of?"

Tommy turned his head sideways and put his finger to his chin. "A bird," he said. "The kind with whaddaya callits." He puffed his hands around his face.

"Plumes," Jo Jo said.

"You're a cutie," Della said, reaching for Tommy, who turned a startled, appalled face to his mother. Jo Jo averted her eyes and Tommy had to suffer a hug.

"Oh, I dread this evening," Della said, settling back on Tommy's bed. "There's actually such a person as a wedding director who's going to lead us through the rehearsal. I don't much like her, but you have to hire her to get married in the Maitland Chapel. I really would have preferred a wedding like yours and Manny's. Remember, Jo Jo? That was such fun. You would have liked it, Tommy. Your dad climbed the Catholic church roof at two in the morning and rang the bell. Then he fell off onto the rectory. Remember, Jo Jo?"

"Vividly. You know, Della, I think I'll try on this alleged matron of honor number for you and see what you think." She escaped into the bathroom and sat on the edge of the tub, her awful dress wadded on her lap. Manny had done so much cocaine at their wedding that he couldn't speak; his throat had gone numb. Everyone had had a good time, it was true, everyone except Jo Jo, who had discovered sometime during the afternoon that she didn't really want to be married. She'd been talking with one of Manny's brothers in Spanish when she suddenly realized that this—standing in the garden of an adobe church, having just wed her boyfriend, wearing a ring, sipping champagne—well, it wasn't the perfect moment. It should have been. She shouldn't have wanted to be anywhere else, doing anything else, but what she imagined was a fast car and a long highway. Weddings had depressed her ever since.

Jo Jo stripped and pulled on her gown. It fell just exactly as it had the day before, lumpy and crooked as something from high school home ec.

She swayed out of the bathroom like a model. "Well?" she said flatly, stopping before Della and Tommy. "No animal comparisons, please."

Della rose and circled her, pulling at the bodice. "Maybe we could rip some of these liner seams apart," she said finally. "That might give you some more room."

"I'm still counting on those flower baskets to cover me."

"You look beautiful, Mom," Tommy lied.

The wedding director was a she-devil. Stu was her apprentice. The two of them fell over one another giving directives to the rest of the party. Della was in tears by the time she'd rehearsed walking down the aisle three or four times.

"I wish my father was still alive," she sniffed to Jo Jo while they waited for the groomsmen to learn their parts. "I'd like him to give me away."

"Your brother will be fine."

"He's shorter than I am."

"So's Stu, Della. You're a tall woman."

"You know, Jo Jo, I bet I wouldn't even be marrying Stu if my father was alive."

"That's interesting."

"It is, isn't it?"

The she-devil was bobbing around near the organ. "Bride?" she called. "Bride?"

Jo Jo joined Tommy in one of the pews.

"Mom, why is Della marrying Stu?" he asked.

"Because it's time, that's why."

"Is that why you married Dad?"

"Nope."

"Why . . ."

A call came out from the altar for matron of honor, and Jo Jo went forward.

At the rehearsal dinner, Della's sister Patsy suggested to Jo Jo in a whisper that the three of them—Della, Jo Jo, and herself—have a little bachelorette party.

"How about in your room?" Patsy said. "I'm sharing with Mom and she's a real wet blanket."

Jo Jo agreed to her room. She prepared by throwing all of her and Tommy's clothes on the shelf of the closet and shutting the door. "Do you suppose we're to drink at this bachelorette party?" she asked her son. "Or what?"

"Tell jokes," Tommy suggested. His job, when his parents threw parties at home, was to set abundant numbers of coasters and ashtrays on every surface. Here, he put carefully folded squares of toilet paper on top of the television and nightstand, ashtrays beside them. When Jo Jo said he could stay with the other kids for a few hours, he'd grabbed her calf with both arms like a humping dog. He promised to go to bed while the women talked.

Patsy showed up wearing a strapless blouse that emphasized her large breasts, both of them. Jo Jo sighed. Families were so hard on one another. "Come in," she said. "Tommy will bring you refreshment." Della trailed in behind her sister. She wore a black T-shirt dress and no shoes.

"I brought peppermint schnapps," Patsy said. "Anybody want a shot?"

Jo Jo and Della both declined. Tommy brought Patsy a glass and she poured herself a four-finger shot. "So what are you doing these days, Jo Jo?" Patsy asked. She sat with her thin legs double crossed, twirling her long hair around her wrist.

"She's a substitute," Tommy told her. He was sitting on his bed, working on crossing his own legs. Grown-ups fascinated him. Della hadn't said a word yet except to thank Tommy for the Coke he brought her. For a while, Jo Jo let Tommy make small talk with Patsy while she and Della sat staring at the peacocks on the bedspreads. Patsy put down one schnapps shot after another.

"Well," Patsy finally said, looking around happily at her fellow bachelorette partiers. "What shall we do on your last single night?"

Della shrugged. "I'm pretty sleepy," she said.

"Nonsense," her sister said, uncrossing her legs and leaning forward. "We should get drunk and play Spin the Bottle." She winked at Tommy. "Little pitcher there will have to go to bed."

"No Spin the Bottle," Jo Jo ruled. "It's my room and I draw the line at Spin the Bottle."

"Play cards," Tommy suggested, softly, so that his mother wouldn't remember he was supposed to be sleeping.

"Poker," Della said, brightening slightly.

"Good idea," Patsy said. "Dealer's choice?"

Jo Jo raised her hands. "You're the bachelorette, Dell, you decide."

"Poker's good. I like poker."

Tommy got his airline deck. Jo Jo dealt first and chose seven-card stud. She won. She rarely didn't win card games. She had card savvy. When Patsy dealt, they played with a number of wild cards, which Tommy loved but which Jo Jo considered something less than adult and barely worth winning. She won again, regardless.

On her turn, Della took the deck into her hands and shuffled sideways, her nail-bitten thumbs going white with the effort. She dealt everyone five cards. "Don't look at them," she commanded, then lifted her own fanned hand, not looking, and flapped it face-forward onto her forehead. "Indian No Peeky," she announced.

Jo Jo smiled, lifting her own cards to her hairline like an Indian headdress.

Tommy could barely contain himself. "You, too!" he told Patsy.

"What a scream!" she said, bowing over in laughter. "How do we bet?" Her cards, at her eyebrows, were all spades.

"You bet your own hand by what everyone else has," Della told her. She read her sister's cards. "Based on what you guys have, I make my move. Got it?"

"I'm in," Jo Jo said carefully, watching Della. There was something quaky in her face, something tenuous and on the verge.

Patsy laughed and laughed. "What a hoot!"

She infected Tommy. "I want to play, I want to play!" He grabbed a fistful of cards from Della and slapped them to his forehead. "Indian No Peeky!" he howled. They never finished the hand; Tommy had to be put to bed, and Patsy was too drunk to keep any of the rules straight. Della's bachelorette party ended fairly early.

It was raining the next morning, a serious storm that had begun in the night, forcing Tommy from his own vast queen-sized bed into Jo Jo's warm one. They woke staring at one another on the same pillow.

"Good morning, Charming Boy."

"Good morning, faithful steed and ally Mom."

"We get free continental breakfast at this joint, you know."

"Did we forget to call Dad last night?" Tommy sat up and fingered the phone next to Jo Jo's bed.

"We didn't forget. We chose to wait until this evening."

"What do you think Dad's doing, Mom? We could call him collect. He always says yes to collect."

Jo Jo looked hard into her son's eyes, then reached past him, picked up the phone after reading the instructions under the glass, and dialed. "Collect, from Tommy," she told the operator, then handed the receiver over.

She stood in the shower debating: was she a bitch, or not? If so, had she always been one, as Manny contended, or had bitchiness come upon her more recently? And if she *hadn't* always been one, what had started it? And finally, where would it all end?

"Dad wants to talk to you," Tommy shouted through the door. Jo Jo put her face under the Water Massage and blew bubbles. Tommy's pounding grew more furious. She switched off the shower and stepped out.

"Tell him to hold his horses," she said.

"He's going to Houston," Tommy yelled.

Jo Jo opened the door and waved Tommy away. She stared at the separate parts of the phone for a moment before lying back on her bed, wrapped in two hotel towels. "Yep?" she said into the receiver.

"It's about time."

"I was in the shower."

"You were stalling in there," Manny said. "I know you well enough."

"What is it? I'm lying here in a towel, freezing my . . ."

Manny guffawed. She heard him exhale something he was smoking.

"What *is* it?" Jo Jo said. "You have ten seconds . . ."

"Don't give me your fucking numbers of seconds. You stay on till I say get off."

Jo Jo took the receiver away from her ear and held it over the cradle. Tommy watched her from the foot of the bed, two fingers in his mouth. It was his comfort habit, something he'd done since he was a baby. He blinked rapidly to quell tears.

Jo Jo put the phone to her ear. She smiled. "Stu's an engineer," she told Manny. "You should see his glasses." Tommy kept watching her. "He seems like a sweet guy."

"Sounds like an asswipe."

"Yes, he is. Very sweet and well mannered. He reminds Tommy of a giraffe."

"Giraffe's asswipe."

"Uh-huh. Tommy tells me you're going to Houston. Again."

"That's right. Again. Don't give me problems. I'm flying out tonight, coming back next week. If you're nice, I'll bring you something."

"Oh, that's not necessary," Jo Jo said, smiling at her son. "You don't have to do that."

"Okay, I won't. Don't forget to turn on the alarm while you're here. I mean it, don't forget." He paused. "You there?"

"Right. Okay."

He laughed, high and blurry. "Hey, Della still a slut?"

"Okay. I will. Me too. Bye-bye." Jo Jo set the phone down, fast, so that Tommy wouldn't hear his father finishing whatever it was he had to say.

Della waited until after the ceremony to disappear, when it was too late, Jo Jo thought. Typical. They'd all, all twenty of them, descended on a seafood restaurant in Decatur, where Jo

Jo spent most of the meal keeping Tommy from throwing his hush puppies in the fish tanks. She had noticed that Stu and Della sat at different tables from one another and that Della was having whispering fits with her younger brother. But Jo Jo hadn't predicted Della's bolting. It impressed her.

After dinner, when all were to join the bride and groom in their hotel room for gift opening, Della simply hadn't turned up. Stu sat on one of the beds with one eye on the door, one eye on the relatives, his and hers, who surrounded him, staring at a mountain of gifts. Sure enough, he had his notebook out, and his pen, ready to record what everyone had gotten them. Jo Jo recalled her own wedding, wrapping paper flying as she and Manny raced through their presents. One of his friends had bought them mudflaps for Manny's truck.

But she got the feeling that Stu was a wrapping-paper saver and that there would be that annoying ritual of running fingernails under tape to keep everything intact. That alone would have driven Jo Jo to desertion, though she could not imagine Della doing the same.

So it was with admiration and surprise that Jo Jo noted her friend's act. When she stood at the hotel room doorway, Tommy in her arms, the eyes of every one of Stu's and Della's families fell upon her and she saw that the role of matron of honor also included, as a minor clause, finding the absent bride.

Tommy wouldn't let her go without him. He was tired of being king of the kids; it was too easy. Jo Jo took him by the hand and made him run to keep up with her long-legged stride.

First they checked the pool and sauna, then the lobby, Jo Jo's room, the parking lot, Della's Volvo. Tommy thought it was a wonderful game. "We should have invited Patsy," he said, breathlessly, as Jo Jo dragged him down a dark corridor between the hotel and the parking lot. "When we find Della, then I'll hide."

"I'll send those other children after you if you do," Jo Jo told him.

"For*get* it."

Back in the hotel, the two of them poked their heads in Stu's room, just to see if she'd returned. Everyone looked up hopefully. Stu's father was singing a hillbilly song to one of Della's nieces, and Stu was fingering the first gift, holding it up to the light and looking underneath. Patsy raised a glass and toasted them. Jo Jo and Tommy raced down the hall to the elevator.

Once they'd gotten on and Jo Jo saw "Bar" over the number seven, she knew she'd find Della. She allowed Tommy to punch the button and up they rode.

But Della wasn't in the bar. A couple sat under a window looking down at the parking lot and the bartender watched the television mounted over his bar.

"Can I come in here?" Tommy asked, toeing the threshold.

The bartender turned. "Sure thing, short stuff."

"We're just looking for someone," Jo Jo said, but Tommy had already climbed up on a stool.

"Soda and soda, maybe chaser of soda?" the bartender asked him.

"Have you seen a woman with really blond hair?" Jo Jo asked him, holding her hands out on either side of her head to indicate frizz.

"Nope." He handed Tommy a glass of soda with two straws, a tiny red umbrella and several garish cherries in it. "No charge."

Tommy gave Jo Jo a sly look. She sat next to him. "A Scotch," she said. "Hold the maraschino."

It was interesting, she had to admit. The weekend had

taken on a whole new appeal since Della had disappeared. Beside her, Tommy said, "You know, Mom, I like this part of the wedding. It's fun running around like crazy." He kicked the bar. "I don't like Stu, do you?" he said.

Jo Jo turned on him suddenly, before he could even catch her eye with his question, and slapped him. "Why," she said, "why do you take such pleasure in other people's pain?" And just as suddenly, again before he could act, she grabbed him to her and held him tight. Smart boy that he was, he gave in easily.

At the elevator, Jo Jo was ready to admit defeat. It disappointed her that she could not find her friend. Her instincts, it seemed, had shut down over the years out of disuse. But just as the elevator bell rang and the doors parted she saw the tasteful hotel sign for the seventh-floor women's room. She yanked Tommy as he started to step forward onto the elevator.

"This way," she said.

The room was quiet, though one stall door was closed. She lifted Tommy in her arms and clamped her hand over his mouth. He had recognized Della's shoes and was about to shout her name. Instead, he and his mother went into the adjacent stall and sat down, he on her lap. He gave her a wide-eyed stare, but was quiet for her.

Della's feet did not move. Jo Jo looked overhead at the sparkly ceiling, at the plush wallpaper on the other side of the stalls. At the cigarette smoke hanging above them.

"Dell," she said. Tommy leaned his cheek to her chest, as if to hear her better. "Dell, I wanted to tell you something yesterday at lunch."

For a second there was nothing and Jo Jo imagined a stranger's voice: "Are you talking to me?" Instead, Della's soft voice came through. "Yeah? Like not to get married?"

"No." Yes, she thought, never give in. "No, I wanted to tell you that I don't remember the hospital. I don't remember coming there and making you laugh."

"What?"

"I think you must be mistaken," Jo Jo said. "It must have been Patsy or somebody else. It wasn't me."

"What?"

"I just told you what."

"Of course it was you, Jo Jo. It was my operation—I can remember. Patsy? Please." She blew smoke into the air and Jo Jo watched it dissipate above her. "Can you believe I actually wore these shoes to my wedding? They're flats, for God's sake."

"It was a nice gesture."

"My father would hate him."

Jo Jo started to tell her no, her father wouldn't hate him, but something in Della's voice made her ask, "You think so?"

"No, not really. My father would have found him *fascinating* or some damn thing."

"He's having a hard time stalling down there without you," Jo Jo said, gently.

"Oh, he is not. He'll do magic tricks. He'll show everybody our wedding notebook and explain how all our friends and relatives are cross-listed alphabetically and by where we met them. You're under 'Grad school, Della.' His great-aunt? 'Maternal family, Stu.' You watch, when we open gifts he's gonna fill in what you got us. He had a fit when he found out you brought Tommy—he didn't know how to reference the little guy. No, Stu won't have any problem entertaining the troops. Hey, Jo Jo?"

"Yeah?"

"Wait here for just a minute. All right?"

"All right."

Della's stall door opened and bounced closed. Then the outer door whooshed open and shut. Around Jo Jo, the bathroom porcelain put out an eerie silence that was almost noise. Tommy settled, snuffling against her silk blouse. "Tell me about Charming Boy," he whispered.

Jo Jo cleared her throat. "The continuing saga of Charming Boy," she began. "Tonight's story finds Charming Boy in the women's room at the Peachtree Inn in Atlanta, Georgia. C.B. has been hot on the trail of a delinquent bride, finally locating her and her cold feet in this unlikely spot . . ."

"His mom helped him."

"With the help of his faithful steed and ally, Mom. But Charming Boy's job is not over yet; he still must convince the bride that she is, indeed, happy, and that there *is* life outside this washroom . . ."

"What's a . . ."

"Bathroom. How will he do it? What if she won't be persuaded? Where will he turn? Who, that's whom, can he trust?"

He ordinarily would have asked for more; it wasn't a very exciting installment, but he was tired from their adventure and only smiled up at her. She jiggled him until his eyes shut. He'd left a wet spot on her shoulder that reminded her of a time when all her clothing had had milky Tommy spots on them. This one made her remember locking him away from her yesterday in their room, slapping him in the bar. She decided that even if Della didn't come back she'd stay in there for a while and let Tommy sleep; she and he had spent plenty of time in bathroom stalls when he was a baby, when Jo Jo didn't feel like nursing him in public. They were quite good at sitting together in bathrooms. But in another moment the door slid open and Della's flats went back into her stall.

"Here," she said, handing a Bloody Mary under the partition to Jo Jo. "This bar is not bad for a hotel. They have celery stalks like palm trees and they let you order 'to go.' "

Jo Jo took her drink, balancing Tommy on one knee.

"Della," she said, after they'd all settled again and she'd had a hearty sip, "tell me about the hospital. What did I say that made you laugh?"

Maggie's Baby

Maggie's baby was eight weeks old. Instead of wobbling like something undecided, his large head now steadied itself over his tiny body. The head was so much more finished looking than the body—eyes blinking thoughtfully, mouth puckering and sucking for Maggie's breast, and the complicated formation of all the shell-like curves around his face—that Maggie knew her baby was certainly decided: he would be here, he seemed to indicate, like it or not. From across the living room his wail came, familiar to Maggie as her own blood beating in her ears. He lay in his bassinet, heaving his chest, turning redder in the face. His intelligent mouth squirmed sideways, opened like a rip, and from it poured his little soul. From her loveseat, Maggie said to him, "That's not you, Tiny, that's just the colic talking." He paused at the sound of her voice, mouth still awry, soul on pause, but then was wracked with another outburst and spilled it into the otherwise quiet room.

Her philosophy had been: he'll cry till he's finished. But that point had not yet been reached. Surely his head contained a memory, she thought, surely he would remember the next day what had not worked the day before. Crying got him nowhere.

Maggie's next tactic had been to satisfy all his possible needs: he ate, he got his diapers changed, he got rocked, held, thumped on the back, dandled, kissed, strolled, walked, bathed, put down, picked up, twirled around. . . And then all over again—could there be anything more? But though he might be still for a moment, his mouth would soon begin its quivering, his eyes their squinting, and his tummy its contracting. He would pull his legs up to himself as if to turn inside out. Maggie would watch in fascination—what would his body do for itself? But apparently it could do nothing satisfactory, and she would end up lifting him again, thumping, dandling, kissing.

Underneath it all ran the ever-present fear that everyone had been right, Maggie was not fit to be a mother, that no teenage girl was. But she believed firmly that if she wasn't fit, then she wouldn't have gotten pregnant. It was as simple as that. She didn't believe in fate, or providence, only that as long as she was physically able she should also be otherwise prepared. It seemed only correct.

The phone, beside her on a twirl-style piano stool, squealed. Maggie looked over at the baby, who quieted promptly at the noise. He turned his head to see through the slats and Maggie let the phone squeal another couple of times just to watch his expression. He didn't make a sound. Finally, reluctantly, she picked up the receiver, spinning the stool with her foot. "Hi, Mom."

"Now how'd you know it was me?" Her mother tried to sound as if she were smiling, Maggie knew, but it didn't come off. She sounded constricted, as usual.

"You always call at noon. It's just one of the things you do."

"Look out the window. I think you'll be able to see me."

Maggie got up and pulled the red and white checked curtains back. Sure enough, there was her mother, across the courtyard, waving coyly from her own checked curtains. "Hi, Mom," Maggie said, flapping her hand as if it were a puppet. Her mother gleefully waved back, mouthing hello.

"How're you two doing today?" her mother said into the

phone, turning away from the curtain. Maggie could see her pat her hair in place from across the courtyard. "I thought maybe we could all go on a walk or something. Or maybe you could come over for supper, I have a little ham and some fresh ears . . ."

"No, I don't think so." Maggie dropped the curtains, unable to watch her mother and talk at the same time. She looked at Tiny, who returned her look without screaming. It was his gift to her, she felt, his complicity: he would not cry while she was on the phone with her mother. At her house—well, that was another story. He would wail his head off at his grand-parents' house. He would only go so far. "Don's coming by and we're going to grill outside."

There was a pause on her mother's end. "Don's coming by?" her mother said. "Now what's he doing coming by?"

"Cooking steaks, if we're lucky, hamburgers if we're not."

"That's not what I mean. I mean . . ."

"I know what you mean," Maggie said. She sat on the piano stool and spun four complete rotations, then stood and kicked it over with a bang.

"What was that?"

"Nothing."

Her mother sighed loudly to indicate she was trying to be nice, aware that it got her nowhere. Maggie repeated that it was nothing, just nothing. She said she had to get off the phone and feed Tiny.

"His name's not Tiny. If you aren't careful, that name will stick and won't he be hot at you later, when all the high school girls call this big galumph 'Tiny.'" Her mother laughed in spite of herself. She had only to think of the future, when Tiny was older, to draw her back into good spirits. "Let me take you two out for an ice cream," she begged. Maggie shook her head, as if the curtains were still open and her mother were watching. "We'll just let Ti . . . Michael have a little taste. He'll love it, I know he will."

"Gotta go, Mom. He's waving his arms and making kissy lips. See you." Maggie grabbed the hang-up button with her finger before her mother could say anything more.

Tiny turned his head upright again and expelled. "Ahh goo," he said, clearly.

Maggie half sat, half lay on the loveseat, Tiny at her breast. He kneed her stomach with both legs when he sucked, pedaling against her. She asked him if he thought he was going somewhere, if he thought he'd been somewhere when he finished one side, and if he thought he started back when he began the other. She loved to nurse. She loved nothing more than lying in the sunlight holding Tiny to her naked breast. It was as if he were trying to reclaim his original place, sucking greedily from where he had been. She loved to feel his eyelashes flitting her sensitive skin, sending miniature waves in all directions. It was thrilling, calming. She had never done anything that felt as right.

She experienced only the vaguest guilt about hanging up on her mother. Really, since the baby arrived she had no time for guilt or her mother. He came first. His crying, his colic, was the only internal alarm she had left. She'd insisted on moving into one of her parents' rental units after the baby was born. Ten little cottages surrounded a larger one, where her mother, father, and older sister still lived. Maggie's bedroom there was still full of stuffed animals, rock and roll posters, glass dancing figurines she'd collected as a girl. The bedspread was frilly, single, covered by a sheer pink canopy. It was a bed that denied sex, that denied having babies (not babies themselves, but *having* them). Its white and gold legs would splinter under her, she was sure, should she ever try to lie there again.

But she was happy to be away, even just across the courtyard, to live in her little house with its miniature refrigerator and hot plate, its Italian-restaurant curtains and loveseat. The walls were panelled pine and reminded her of the cozy inside of a nut. It was a sturdy cottage with strong brass locks. When she and Vanessa were little, they'd played house in the vacant cottages. Vanessa was always Dad, smoking a Lincoln Log cigar and demanding dinner (Play-Doh carrots, pork chops); afterwards, bouncing on the saggy mattress and box springs. Now, Maggie had a small TV for when Tiny slept.

He opened his mouth at her, smiling in contentment. This would last only a few moments. Then the gas would kick in. But for now he smiled, showing the empty spaces where his teeth would be, the pink skin that would curve around them. His nose, Maggie had decided, would be slightly too big for his face, like Don's, but his eyes, large and long-lashed, would make up for it. He spit her nipple out, bringing both legs up under himself. Quickly she shifted him, holding his tummy hard on her shoulder. For a moment he was too startled to cry, but then he remembered his pain and howled with renewed resource. Maggie, renewed herself, patted him with the flat of her palm. The pads from her bra lay beside her like two soft saucers.

She ate Manhattan clam chowder and listened to him cry. She washed her few dishes with the water turned full force, incorporating his voice like an extra faucet. She swept with the vacuum, though nothing was dirty enough to merit it. She opened her American history book and read about George Washington Carver, proving to herself she could do it without letting Tiny bother her. She yelled in to him that he would appreciate peanut butter someday. She ate an Eskimo pie so slow it melted sticky white and brown drops on her wrist and hand.

His crying was of a particular inflection. He cried steadily, as if monitoring his energy consumption, saving it and using it wisely. He cried almost mechanically, as if it were his job; however useless he may have considered it, he continued dutifully. He cried as if that were how he breathed.

Maggie's pediatrician, the same man who'd taken care of her when she was little, did not approve of her being a mother. No one really approved, but he disapproved more. He acted as if colic were Maggie's just deserts. He said he usually recommended rides in the car, but seeing as she had no car . . . He'd shrugged. Maggie told him you didn't have to have a car in order to be a mother. He said that was certainly an understatement. She told him there was nothing to do now but help her, that it was too late to be ashamed of her. He said he wasn't ashamed but that it wasn't too late. After that, Maggie relied on the nurses from the hospital who'd been there when Tiny was born, the two of them childless but so knowledgeable you'd never guess it. They taught her to carry Tiny on his tummy like a football clutched to her side.

She had not known what to expect from her parents. Her mother was not so bad, but every time she was around there was only one way to do things. You laid babies on their stomachs (though Tiny wailed louder that way), you fed for only ten minutes on a side (though Tiny clung furiously for more), you put babies to bed at seven-thirty to allow yourself your own life (though Maggie wanted no other life and Tiny was still wide awake and howling at seven-thirty). Maggie was close enough to childhood herself to remember what she'd promised she would never do. There would be no bedtimes. There would always be a place to make a mess. They would decide together what to have for supper. They would listen to music often.

"You can hang whatever pictures you like in your room," she promised Tiny now, leaning over to investigate his diaper.

It was yellow around the edges. "And you can stick stickers to your headboard. And you can get a cat." Tiny squinted as if questioning her promises. He stopped crying long enough for her to lift him to the coffee table. "And you can play with yourself," she added, as he reached for his exposed penis. It bobbed sweetly under his clawing fingers, pink and smooth like a button.

Maggie did not love Tiny's father, though at their high school that was supposed to be a prerequisite for going all the way. But she had enjoyed making love. In fact, she still enjoyed it. Don wanted them to get married, to live in her parents' rental unit, to finish high school as a couple, but Maggie was content to live on her leave of absence by herself. She'd already played house in these cottages. She didn't love Don, just sex with Don. And Tiny. She loved Tiny. He was, she thought, the only person she knew she loved. If she wanted to know if she loved anyone else, she would have something to measure against.

At three-thirty Maggie's older sister Vanessa got home from school. She pulled her pastel lawn chair into the courtyard and stared up at the sky, shielding her eyes with her palm. She was eighteen, graduating this month. Up until last Christmas she'd been in constant panic over being a virgin. She couldn't bear the thought that her little sister had made it before she did. No more. Just a few days earlier she'd confessed to Maggie that she would wait.

"Till you're married?" Maggie had said, shocked.

"Well . . ." Vanessa trailed off, casting a quick glance at Tiny, then at Maggie's shirtfront, where two wet spots had formed over her breasts.

"There's such a thing as birth control," Maggie said.

"Tell me about it," Vanessa had answered. When Maggie

was pregnant, losing her waist and outgrowing her clothes, Vanessa had quit confiding in her. For her part, Maggie suddenly felt both younger and older than her sister. She was sometimes acutely ashamed of herself; other times, she felt only anger with her sister. Lately, they hadn't had much to say to one another.

Vanessa stretched, lowered herself onto the recliner, and lifted a magazine to her flat bronze stomach. She reached down distractedly and snapped her bikini bottom on either side. While Maggie watched, her mother came out of the house with a load of wet laundry slung on her hip. As she hung clothes, she talked to Vanessa, who wouldn't look up from her magazine. The laundry, mostly bed sheets from the day rentals, eventually formed a wavering white wall between Maggie and her old house, her old family behind it.

Her father came to visit her every afternoon after he got home from work. He refinished furniture. Everybody wanted old oak furniture these days, and they wanted it natural. It used to be that he only worked on the rentals, replacing plumbing and painting walls, but eventually all the major work was done and the most he needed to do now was install a new set of box springs or change a lock. He and his friend Hal, who'd lived in number two since Maggie was born, rented a garage a few blocks away to refinish in. He smelled of cut wood, of sawdust. His hands, now rocking Tiny back and forth before him, sure and reliable after two babies of his own, were blunt and scabbed. He was forever hurting his hands.

"How's the Moose?" he said. He wanted Tiny to play football. That seemed simple enough to Maggie, so she didn't object.

"A whiner," Maggie said. She watched Tiny's chest, surrounded by her father's huge hands. His little face was curious.

Her father set Tiny back in his bassinet—a gift from Hal—
and took the clam juice on ice Maggie offered him. At the
kitchen table, he looked peacefully around the room, as he did
every night. His visits had begun in the hospital and continued once Maggie came home. Despite Tiny's wailing, he
liked visiting them. He and Maggie talked about beautiful
houses and remodeling ideas. For redoing her cottage, they
always knocked out the wall between the kitchen and the living room first. But from there, their plans diverged: install
solar panels, her father might say. Maggie always voted for a
patio and more windows. At one time the two of them wanted
to convert the whole group of cottages into a sort of mini-
mall, where artists could rent them to sell their work.

Tonight when her father popped his knuckles the skin on
one cracked open and started to bleed. He held it to his mouth
while Maggie got a bandage. He mumbled something when
she came back.

"What?"

"I said, 'Your mother wants you to come to supper.' "

"Well, only if I can bring Don," Maggie said, "and you know
that's out. So, no thank you." She calmly patted the bandage
in place, noting all the other notches and scrapes he hadn't
bothered to cover.

"I'm just the delivery man with the message," he said,
"that's all. It's all right with me if Don comes. I like Don." He
wiped his upper lip of clam juice.

"I know you do," Maggie said.

"He's a part of the family, far as I'm concerned." Her father
was the only one who thought so. He was the only adult,
Maggie thought, of the whole lot. Don's mother had pushed
for an abortion; she was modern. Maggie's mother voted for
adoption and private school. Don's father had no opinion except that Don was a fool for getting into this situation. Don's

sisters were both so young their opinions didn't count. And Maggie's sister had changed her mind about virginity. But Maggie's father had been different.

"Sure, I know that," Maggie said. "It's just, you know . . ." She shrugged. Tiny, who'd been snuffling for several minutes, now burst into tears, whinnying full force.

"If it were up to me, he'd be here right now," her father went on, over the crying. "I like the guy."

"I'm going to feed Tiny," Maggie said, knowing her father appreciated the advance notice. He didn't like to be around when her breasts were loose.

"Okay then, I'll be seeing you later." He stood and held the hand with the bandage out. "Thanks for the first aid. And the clam sauce."

Back on the loveseat, Maggie let Tiny nurse on one side until the sun set, leaving the room dark and warm. She lifted him and resettled him and let him search for the other breast by himself, kissing all around until he latched on, then pulling hard. Maggie shut her eyes and smiled, felt deep tugs at her stomach and then lower. They made her want something—but what? She felt almost like crying—but not quite. There was something, she felt sure, something as of yet undiscovered she could do, that would satisfy that desirous tug.

Don squeaked the door open and peered into the dark room. He didn't want to wake Tiny, should Tiny be sleeping. Maggie was just buttoning her blouse, the baby held over the crook of her arm. Don was seventeen, one year older than Maggie, though he seemed to her ages behind her. When he held Tiny he giggled nervously, always ready to return the baby to her. She thought of her father's hands, big and sure.

"Hey," Don said. He stood over the two of them, staring at Maggie's mouth. "Let me turn on a light, will you?"

"Sure." Maggie straightened up, pulling her legs under her. Tiny was so full he was drunk, happy and lazy. Don snapped on the light and sat next to them.

"Want to hold him?" Maggie asked.

"That's okay. He's asleep anyway." Don folded his arms over his chest. "I brought lamb chops."

"Lamb chops?"

"Yes, I thought you'd like them. And there was a deal on at Kroger's. We'll barbecue, just like steaks. You'll love them, Mag, I know you will."

She smiled.

Don looked around the room. "So. Whatcha been doing?"

"Nothing," she said. "How about you?"

"Nothing here, either." He waited a second, then hopped up and went into the kitchen, snapping on more lights. Since Maggie had told him she didn't want to get married, he'd been unsettled whenever he came over. He didn't know how he fit in, he said. Tiny cried when he held him, and he and Maggie didn't have much to say to each other because she didn't really like to talk about babies or Tiny and that was the only thing left they had in common. When he found out she was pregnant he'd kept his distance for a few months. Then, some time after she'd taken her leave from school, he'd come around again, tutoring her in algebra and rubbing her shoulders. For a while they quit making love; Maggie felt he was paying penance. They studied and they never talked about what would happen after the baby was born.

"My mother got a new car," Don said from the kitchen. "Maybe we'll get a baby seat and go for a spin." A spice bottle crashed to the floor, then another. "Sorry," Don called. "You think lemon pepper would be good on lamb chops?"

"I guess so." Tiny had fallen asleep across her arms, dangling as if dead. Maggie had to resist the temptation to wake him, to make sure he was still breathing. His chin was covered with a filmy cottage cheeselike substance, something his stomach did to her milk. She laid him in the bassinet and covered him with an ABC blanket Don's mother had given her.

Dinner ended up in bed. They'd cooked outside, moving the grill to the front so as to be out of view of her parents' house, and sat eating potato chips while the lamb chops sizzled. There was only one patio chair and Maggie had sat on Don's lap, Tiny sleeping in his bassinet beside them. They faced the street, watching people walk or drive by. Maggie thought she recognized some freshmen from school. They were almost sophomores, she thought. She looked down at sleeping Tiny and decided she'd gotten somewhere over the school year, too. Meanwhile, Don had accomplished an erection beneath her. They went inside.

Their plates, with only a lamb chop centered on each, they balanced on their naked stomachs, resting against the headboard of Maggie's bed. The bed was a sturdy double, its headboard an unattractive but functional bookcase full of paperbacks Maggie had taken to reading at night. In the corner was Tiny's crib. He flailed in his sleep as his mother made love. She was hungry for sex, she discovered. She wanted Don to be . . . what? More. It was all she could come up with. She wanted him to mean more to her than he did. But sex was nice, peaceful. It satisfied something anxious inside her. She wished she could start the process all over again when it was over, feel the release once more. But Tiny was crying now, his nap over, his stomach upset.

Don kissed both her breasts before Tiny got to them, then went to do the dishes while Maggie lounged naked on her tangled sheets, feeding the baby.

Don never spent the night, which was okay with Maggie; she didn't want him to start thinking he lived with her. Plus, he and his parents would have had difficulty greeting one another in the mornings—Don arriving home just in time to change clothes and get to school, the two of them on their way out the door for work.

In the kitchen, Don clattered and banged. He'd left his jeans and shirt beside the bed, inside out on the floor. After a while he stepped quietly into the room. Maggie pretended to sleep, making herself go limp against the headboard, arms only loosely around the baby. Don got dressed quickly, hobbling out the bedroom door with only one high-top tennis shoe on. Just as she started to open her eyes, he came back in. But he hadn't noticed she was really awake. He was staring at Tiny, and it was Tiny whose head he bent over to kiss before he left.

Maggie got up. She stretched in front of the mirror, pinching the small roll of extra stomach she still had around her waist. She dressed and went through the house turning off lights, locking the doors. Across the courtyard, she could see her family's kitchen light, their heads as they moved from the television to the refrigerator. Vanessa's bedroom was lighted, the shapes of her furniture foggy through her sheer curtains. Maggie imagined her at her desk, writing in her laborious beautiful handwriting all about cell division and DNA. Vanessa would be a nurse, would be going off to school next year to become one. There was nothing in that to envy, Maggie told herself, her forehead against the cool pane of glass. She closed the curtains, certain that she was only momentarily nostalgic, and returned to her bedroom.

On most days, Maggie had any number of things she could do. For her mother, she cleaned the overnight rentals, changing sheets and scrubbing toilets. She took Tiny with her. She also brought a radio and sang along with the country western songs. Someday she would move South and take singing lessons. She would sing backup first, then eventually move on to being a lead singer in a small, unknown, opening-act sort of group, eventually to be discovered and sent on a tour of her own. It would take a long time, but she was realistic and knew that. "Love is a rose," she sang to Tiny, "but you better not pick it, it only grows when it's on the vine . . ."

After cleaning, she might wheel Tiny over to the park and watch the ducks. Or she might get into a conversation with another mother whose baby sat in a stroller similar to Tiny's, its face just as placid and bored as his. She and the mother might talk about the ducks, but most often the other mother talked about her husband or her older children. It wasn't so bad, because she usually made Maggie aware of how fortunate she was not to have those others.

In the afternoons she came home to her little house. Some days, when Tiny's crying took up more room than she could bear, Maggie opened the door and left. She made herself walk around the block, admiring the flower garden at the end of the street, navigating through the tricycle clutter, hollering amiably at barking dogs. He would still be there, she told herself, forcing her pace to be slack. Her house would be there and he would be in it, wailing just as he had when she'd gone out, not three minutes before.

Otherwise, she fed Tiny. She watched bad game shows or read books. She thought about her friends and her sister in school. She contemplated the future. There didn't seem to be anything she couldn't do. For instance, even now, Tiny lying crying on the bed. Maggie pulled her shirt over her head and flung it to the floor as if it had attacked her. She reached behind herself and unfastened her thick-strapped, old-lady bra, shucking it as well. Straddling her son, her rump lifted and swinging in the air, she dangled her swollen breasts over his face. His crying subsided only momentarily; when he discovered she wasn't going to slow their pendulumlike movement for him, he roared.

Maggie lifted her behind, lowered her breasts, swung them like the sharp blade from a James Bond movie, closer, closer. Nipples grazed Tiny's lips, nose. Flesh slapped his cheeks. In a moment the weight of her breasts, their fullness, closed down over him like night.

There was no sound. There was nothing. Her baby's hands had flattened palm up to either side, as if waiting for something small to be placed in them. His eyelids did not flutter.

Maggie's own heart stopped—not even a second, not long enough for her to panic, not long enough for her to lose him— just long enough to right itself, the way a sharp breath will sometimes cure hiccups.

Beneath her mouth the shape of his nose and lips was unfamiliar, as foreign and incomprehensible as his head had once been, passing from her body.

Into him she breathed slowly, yet with the assurance of success. She felt she could see deep inside him, his small heart and ribs, her own breath filling him. She imagined his life rushing back to him from her—she had only borrowed it for a second, he could now have it back. After not even half a minute, he lifted his hands. He clutched her hair around his face and pulled, angry and strong. They cried together loudly, forcefully—as if breaking in new lungs. They reminded Maggie of times when she and Vanessa were children, when their sorrow had such power as to infect one another, neither, eventually, able to remember what their tears had been for.

The Expendables

At one end of the block a funeral was being held and at the other end a wedding would begin in an hour. It was ironic: at our house people were arriving dressed like ice cream cones, pastels and sorbets (the tuxedo I'd rented was called Chocolate), bearing gifts wrapped in silver and lavender, while down the street you never saw so much navy and black. Beginnings and endings. This corner and that.

My sister Yvonne was marrying Chris the Sicilian. Our family had its doubts. Only a month ago Chris had sold one of my brothers a Cadillac for a song. Mint condition, 1964, black interior of leather. Well, not quite mint; there were the holes along the side—bullet holes or repair holes, depending on who told the story. And the fact that the test drive took place at three in the morning, around the graveyard at St. Augustino's. But my sister had been married before; everyone fell back on that for reassurance: this time she knew what she was doing. Her first husband, Mark, modeled and waited tables, and would have been perfect except that he was better looking than Yvonne. I think he weighed less, too, by the time they divorced, though they were still friendly. He was here today, helping my mother with the buffet; she didn't know what to do with some of the unattractive dishes Yvonne's roommates had contributed to the party. Mark told her he had a feeling for aesthetics. He would find some way to "elegantize" the eggplant and squash.

My beat was car parking, which I got by saying I wanted to serve drinks. My brother Leon, who'd begged to park cars, now circulated, asking guests to name their poison. We'd worked this out last night. Every time we met we slugged down a Kamikaze each. Our Uncle Cy was mixing everything in plastic champagne glasses, and the Kamikaze, served in a glass with such circumference, carried a powerful nose.

A good many of the guests were neighbors. Our family, whom my father called "Catholic only in theory and size," had lived here twenty-six years. We knew everybody, including the Gypsies on the corner, the ones having the funeral. There'd been a large debate about inviting them. They hadn't lived in the neighborhood long enough to be automatic guests. Plus, they insisted on painting their house Pepto-Bismol pink every spring. It's embarrassing to have to admit that my family would discriminate on such a basis, but it's dishonest to say that they didn't. It wasn't just the paint (every spring, for God's sake). A year, even in Chicago, couldn't do enough damage to merit a painting that often. It was the furniture on the lawn, or what used to be the lawn.

One of the first things the Gypsies did when they moved in was pave their front yard in big concrete squares. Then they set up a sofa and a bunch of chairs and a table. They spent a great deal of time out there, not really talking, not socializing exactly, just sitting and watching the street. The men stood on the corner, also not talking, most of the day. I'd see them when I went to school; they'd be there when I got back. They broke for dinner around six, then reassembled, toothpicks in their mouths, about seven. The Gypsies had become a neighborhood landmark now, something I pointed out to friends I brought home for the first time. I'd show them the house with the swastikas in the rock work, explaining that before Hitler they meant good luck, then the Gypsies' pink house, the clan out front relaxing on their furniture as if a TV game show was on in front of them, pleasantly numbed and distracted.

But today I saw no one on the furniture; in fact, the couch had disappeared altogether. The men, however, still stood on the corner, all in their suits and bow ties. One of them was tuning a violin, the nee-no, nee-no of catgut on catgut carrying down the block. The oldest man, I guess the grandfather, and I had a waving relationship so I waved today, smiling slightly at both of us in our monkey suits. He just nodded in my direction, his head heavy, it seemed.

The car I was waiting for was my Cousin Gerita's. She drove an orange Spitfire that I was dying to park. We'd already used up the curbs on both sides of the street, so I would have to take it to St. Augustino's and park in their lot. Two blocks; out of sight of the house; me and the Spitfire. I'd take Leon if he was convenient. I was only sorry we had to have the wedding at our house. If this had been Yvonne's first wedding, we'd be at St. Augustino's and nobody'd notice if I was there or not. Me and the Spitfire and an hour to kill.

But it was my father's business partner, Mr. Payton, who showed up next. His tie, though he was old and infirm, was thin and leather and silver. His wife wore a silk turquoise pantsuit that washed around her like so many scarves in a breeze. "Daniel," Mr. Payton coughed out to me, as if proving he could so remember names, bowing his head once while he pressed the warm key to his Lincoln in my hand. He'd separated it from his fat ring of other keys, as if I'd race over and rob his house, given the chance. He didn't even break stride. He was doing crooked things with money from his and my father's hotel business, but nobody'd been able to prove anything. The whole affair gave my father ulcers. As I navigated the Paytons' tub of a car to the church, I remembered it was at one of Mr. Payton's hotel functions that Yvonne had met Chris-the-probable-Mafioso.

When I got back, there were three other cars double-parked outside our house, the third one Gerita's. She'd washed it for the occasion. Its eyeball headlights shone. Gerita was leaning on the car she'd parked in front of, thin legs crossed at the ankles. Her dress was a silly bright yellow, but she looked great anyway.

"Hey, Cruiser. Nice tie." She reached up as if to straighten it and I looked down. She flipped me on the nose. "Gotcha."

"Leon's serving drinks," I told her.

"And doing a damn fine job." She nodded to the hood of the car she leaned on. Three Kamikazes waited. "Do me a favor and park my baby before you belt these down, huh Danny?"

"Who came in the other two cars?" I said.

Sighing, she waved a finger in the air. "A fart. His mother. Her sister. Another fart. Several brats. You think Yvonne will stay married this time?"

"Why not?"

"Good enough. Hope springs eternal. By the way, did I mention I like your tie?" She smiled and I made as if to look down again, nodding my head up in time for her to miss my nose. "I think you're quicker drunk than not," she said, heading with an exaggerated swagger for the house.

St. Augustino's lot was filling with our party's cars. Some people didn't wait for me to park them, just drove over themselves. I watched the people I didn't know unload, but they didn't look like Mafia to me. They looked, if it was possible, duller even than my relatives. Whenever I got in a group like that, a group of sort of middle-aged people with little kids, all wearing basically the same thing, I started thinking, *This group is expendable.* I don't even know where it came from. I would get it riding the El or standing around in a department store or in the waiting room at the doctor's. A group like that could vanish from the face of the earth and nobody'd notice. That's what I'd think. The problem, of course, is that there I was, trapped among the expendables.

I ran back to the house, dying to get into the Spitfire, but cars were starting to pile up. My heart dropped when I saw my mother standing at the curb looking up and down the block, I presumed for me.

"Let Leon help me," I told her, but she scowled, as if I'd addressed her in German.

"What's going on over there?" she said, aiming her glare down the block.

"Funeral."

"Whose?"

I shrugged. "Where's Leon?"

"How do you know it's a funeral?"

"I saw the casket."

"They got a casket there? In the house? What do they mean having a funeral at home?" She hardly paused before lighting into me. "What are these drinks doing on Cy's car? Did you put these here, Daniel? Alcohol can ruin a car's finish. You should know that. I see Princess Gerita made it."

"Be nice."

"*You* be nice—you don't touch those drinks." She stared at them evilly, tempted, I could tell, to dump them. This wedding would give her ulcers. She and my father would have a matched set. She loved Yvonne's first husband. She'd adopted him, hoping for a reconciliation, a reprieve at the last minute. Yvonne hadn't told her that Mark was gay, that he'd already found a new lover. My mother is a person you can't imagine breaking this sort of news to. So Yvonne told her they didn't spark. Period. With Chris, there was spark. There was lightning. That was probably what my mother objected to, all the electricity the two of them set off.

Yvonne's roommates pulled up and I cringed along with my mother, though we'd both seen their car plenty of times. They'd hand-painted an old Falcon purple and gold. Over the hood was an enormous silver cross. Other identifiable shapes dotted a landscape of gold clouds and purple hills. A rainbow broke in half when the passenger door opened. Neither of my sister's roommates had a driver's license or insurance, and whenever they parked they always left the key in the ignition. They'd once told me they believed responsibility had to come from within.

"You put that car somewhere out of sight," my mother hissed, turning for the house before Jennifer or Cleo stepped out.

Jennifer, tall and humorless, didn't say a word to me as she passed. It was because I refused to call her Cassandra, which was her witch name. No joke—she thought she was a witch. But Cleo gave me a pat on the shoulder. "It's very exciting, isn't it? I love weddings." She had flowers pinned all over her.

After I parked their car and the four others that had kept me from the Spitfire, I looked around to make sure neither Gerita nor my mother was in sight, and shot the Kamikazes down. I'd made Gerita promise me that if, God forbid, she died, she'd leave me her car. She'd told me that if she died, God willing, it would be *in* her car and she wouldn't leave anything recognizable for the living.

As I was adjusting the seat and the radio and the window and the gearshift and finally the rearview, I saw the Gypsies. They were coming down the street, lined up like a parade, the coffin rolling along on a wagon. I turned in the seat, willing them to disappear. They were coming my way, to St. Augustino's, of course, but that isn't what I thought of immediately. My first impression was that they were descending on me like an army, slowly but inevitably. When I was a kid, that's how Yvonne would chase me, not fast, but terribly slow, her feet falling like thuds of doom behind me.

I revved the Spitfire and took off with a squeal. I didn't mean to, it wasn't to show off. I just wanted to get away from the Gypsies. I didn't want to ruin their procession; I didn't want them to ruin my drive. But before I got to the end of the next block, there was Chris, sauntering with his groomsmen toward our house. Their silver tux jackets flapped in the wind and they passed a bottle among them. Chris was football-player big and so were his friends. Dressed alike, as they were, they looked like a team headed for victory. I honked and, after some confusion on Chris's part about where the noise had come from—for an instant his face had taken on a hard, aggressive, fuck-you kind of look before he saw who it was—he waved me down.

I checked the rearview again. Sure enough, there, reaching the end of our block, were the Gypsies, a bigger but less authoritative team, making their way our way. This was the end of my Spitfire ride, cut short before I'd even lost sight of my house. To make things worse, curb space had opened not ten yards in front of me. I made the best of parallel parking—shifting the full pattern each time between reverse and first—and then climbed reluctantly out, remembering to leave the radio at full force for Gerita to ignite to.

"Dan-*yell!*" Chris hooted. "What's the story with these yahoos?"

"Funeral," I said. My encounters with Chris were always tinged with my fear that he would find something to dislike about me and then punch me in the nose for it. Not that he'd ever touched me. Not even that he wouldn't recover quickly—

the next time he saw me, he'd have completely forgotten what he'd disliked before. We'd start fresh. Clean slate. But then I'd be just as likely to show my flaw again, get punched once more.

"What?"

"A funeral. Someone has passed on." The procession waited at the corner for the cross traffic to clear. They didn't pile up, but instead stayed in parade formation. I heard violins.

"Passed on what?" his best man said. They all laughed, stomping around one another and wiping their mouths. My mother's new ulcers had a hard day to look forward to. The bottle they drank from was cherry vodka. Cherry vodka! I almost laughed. He probably *was* Mafia; who else could be seen in public with such a dopey drink.

The Gypsies crossed the street, one man on either side of the procession holding a flat, no-nonsense hand up to stop traffic. Please God, I prayed, don't let this become a scene. Though I fell back on it frequently, prayer had never done me any good. Today it failed, as always. Chris's gang of tuxedoed hoodlums began whooping.

"Come on guys," I said in the direction of the Gypsy grandfather. He was close enough that I could see his right eyelid twitter; he'd heard me. And, lucky me, Chris had not. I'd separated myself from him and his friends by staring, perplexed, at the houses on the other side of the street, as if trying to remember an address.

"Nice duds, dude," one of Chris's team said.

"Which one's the corpse?"

"Don't you guys know 'Beer Belly Polka'?"

The Gypsies, with the exception of the grandfather's eyelid, showed no sign of having heard them. They faced St. Augustino's and plodded on as if they wore blinders. The coffin seemed small to me, the way the mummies at the Field Museum seemed small: it was hard to imagine a human fitting the confines. Obviously, someone in the group had made the coffin: its grain was rough and there were knotholes, like two big brown misaligned eyes, facing me. At the rear of the group were the musicians, two violins and a huge bass. The music was weepy and too slow; I imagined baying hounds and tearful women. Chris's friends extended their left arms at their chins and sawed—air violins. Two little boys carried the bass, stooped over and scooting backwards like crabs, while a fat woman played, her arms circling the instrument. They were admirably coordinated.

"What a fucking blimp," Chris said, as the woman passed. She was the end of the parade. Her buttocks rolled under her faded black dress like the haunches of a rhino. I sighed, relieved they'd gotten by without incident.

"I'm about to become a married man!" Chris yelled at their backs. "Let's not have any more dying today, got it?"

Back at the party, Yvonne was explaining her philosophy to Gerita. "Every few years you have to change your life," she said. "I think about who I was the last time I got married—it's like a whole nother person. Remember? I was blond." Yvonne now had wiglike black hair, dry and frazzled, cut in the shape of Cleopatra's.

"But it's not just hair," Yvonne told Gerita. "One day I woke up and decided I wasn't happy being who I was. So I changed." She'd dropped out of college, begun steadily gaining weight, divorced Mark, moved in with the witch and the midwife. "You just have to set your mind and change," she told Gerita, wide-eyed with wonder at the simplicity of it.

"I change my life every day," Gerita said. "You think I would have worn something this subdued to a wedding yesterday?" She looked around at the pastels, rolling her eyes at me.

"Yvonne," I said. "Your husband and his henchmen hath arrived." Chris and the group had gotten sidetracked at the door, slapping backs with the rest of the men relatives, but I still felt responsible for delivering them into someone else's jurisdiction.

"Oh," Yvonne said, leaving us.

"If he's Mafia," Gerita said, "why didn't his family throw the party? Now, *that* would have been interesting."

Leon joined us, a silver tray of empty plastic glasses on his upturned palm. "If they don't start this soon, Uncle Cy will embarrass us badly. You can bet on it. He's looped." Leon's voice broke and he giggled. "More looped than even me. What's the delay?"

"It's the damned harpist," my mother said, from behind Gerita. My mother was always sneaking up on people. She liked to pretend she was all-knowing. "Yvonne's damned harpist is over forty-five minutes late."

"Pardon her French," I said to Gerita.

My mother smacked me on the arm. "Go get your sister in here. I'm tired of entertaining her friends." I looked around at the people surrounding us. None of them were Yvonne's friends; they were neighbors, strangers, relatives. They weren't anybody's friends. Expendables.

Gerita and Leon and I found Yvonne in the grape arbor out back. It was badly overgrown with dead vines and weeds, and its floor was covered with fallen paint chips. We used to have two porch swings hung facing each other in the arbor. Our family used to eat dessert there in the summer. I'd had enough to drink to be nostalgic about it, back when Leon's feet couldn't reach the ground and when Milo was still on speaking terms with my father. Yvonne had been a quiet brown-haired girl with a clever sense of humor. She always knew exactly what you meant when you said something. She'd let you know when she caught your eye.

She and her bridesmaids, Jennifer and Cleo, and her ex-husband Mark, sat cross-legged on the dirty floor. A fake-antique Pears Soap tray was in front of them, complete with gold tube, razor, and coke-filled Baggie. Yvonne looked up at us and smiled. Was it possible that her eyes had slid farther apart on her face since she was little? For a moment I couldn't reconcile the two girls, the sister from my childhood and the sister of today's wedding. "Tootsky?" she said.

"Yeah!" Leon dropped immediately to the floor.

"Pass," Gerita said, though she also sat down.

"Mother wants to know where your harpist is," I said.

"Your *damned* harpist," Gerita corrected.

Leon giggled again. He was leaning over the tray trying to manipulate a line up his nose.

"Sit," Mark said to me. "You're so tall when you're standing." I squatted next to Cleo, who immediately reached out and patted my penny loafer. She was a person who just naturally touched everyone around her. It was very reassuring. I thought suddenly, If we could just get rid of Jennifer, I wouldn't mind living with these five people. We could be very happy. How lucky I was, to know five people I liked well enough to live with.

"That's better," Mark said, smiling dreamily.

"Wouldn't it be nice if we could just sit out here all afternoon, just the bunch of us?" Yvonne said, looking at me. It was as if she'd read my mind. I felt better, believing she might have something left of her childhood self in her somewhere.

"Mm hmm," Cleo said.

Only Jennifer seemed to disagree. She was scowling down at the part in Leon's hair as he took a second line. It was probably her coke and now she saw it going to waste on my little brother.

"You look awfully pale," Mark said to Yvonne.

"It's true," Cleo said. "Have you been taking your potassium?"

"She's getting married," Gerita said. "She's got a right to be pale."

"To sing the blues," Leon sang.

"It's her hair," I said. "It's so black she looks pasty. But good."

"We'll rouge you before the big event," Mark told Yvonne. "We'll rouge you good."

"My mother wishes you were marrying me again," she said, sighing, dropping her plump hands into her lap.

"I'll tell her I'm sterile. That'll set her straight."

"You are?" Leon sat back, his eyes blinking slowly, like a doll's. If we weren't careful, he would pass out. "You aren't?"

"Only the shadow knows." Mark pulled the tray from Leon. "Talk to me, Miss Pears."

"That's my line," Leon whined.

"No, your line is, 'RA hah hah hah hah.' "

Leon rolled onto his back laughing and then stayed that way, staring absently up at the twisted vines of the arbor roof.

Yvonne turned to her roommate. "I wish you had your Runes, Cassandra. I'd like to know how today will be."

"I always have my Runes." Jennifer said, glumly. She pulled a red velvet bag from a larger mesh bag beside her and began shaking it. Rocks rattled inside. Yvonne pulled one out.

"Well?"

"A portentous day to wed," Jennifer said, turning the rock over in her hand.

"Portentous," Leon echoed thoughtfully.

"Oh, good," Yvonne said, smiling brightly. Mark and I exchanged glances.

"Will she stay married?" Gerita asked. "Ask if she'll stay married."

"Will I stay married?" Yvonne turned her hopeful, over-made-up eyes to Jennifer. Another stone was extracted.

"Neither yes nor no."

"How can that be?"

Jennifer shrugged. She reached into the bag herself and

pulled out three rocks, laying them before her quickly. "There's a dark element involved in this wedding. I'm sorry, Yvonne, but that's what the stones say." She didn't look sorry. Bad news seemed to brighten her.

"It's the Gypsy funeral," I said. "They marched by our house and left a shadow."

"Ask it will Wrigley Field ever get lights," Leon said, still on his back. "Wouldn't you love a night game?"

Eventually we had to drift in. We heard harp music.

The harpist was a woman in her fifties who worked with Yvonne at the bar. She had a big happy mouth that moved along with the music she was playing. I missed most of the ceremony because I was in charge of Leon, who kept insisting we were in heaven. He tottered around the foyer, signing the guest list now and then. I had too many sets of car keys in my pockets to be comfortable sitting anyway. When the first relatives emerged weeping from the living room, I hustled Leon out the front door. It was time for a spin in the Spitfire.

The sun was behind St. Augustino's now, casting a peculiar burnt orange shadow down the length of the block. The day had cooled since I'd last been out.

Leon waited until I'd opened his door and helped him aim his long legs into the passenger side footspace before he told me he couldn't possibly go for a ride.

"Why not? We'll roll down the window, cool your jets."

He shook his head emphatically. "I'll be ill," he said somberly, then belched. "Very ill."

I leaned back in the seat and hit the steering wheel with my palms. "You won't be ill," I said.

"I'll retch," he said. "Just smelling the inside of the car is making me queasy."

"How about around the cemetery? I won't go fast."

"I warned you," he said, raising his hands in a shrug.

I shouldn't have, but I started the engine anyway. We had only a little while before we'd be missed. I'd forgotten about leaving the radio on and it screamed out at us, making my heart jump.

"Don't think about your stomach," I yelled to Leon, over the engine and rushing air. We whizzed around the side and back lot of St. Augustino's and into the graveyard. Thousands of black crows took flight at the sound of the engine and thousands more when I began honking the horn. Because I'd learned to drive in the cemetery, with and without permission, I could have driven it with my eyes closed. The roadway was one lane and curved through the various sections of dead people the way I imagined the German autobahn cutting through that country. Everywhere we drove, crows flew out in waves before us, as if from the sheer power of the Spitfire's engine. It was dark enough to turn on the headlights, but I liked driving in the dusk. I felt I could actually be headed somewhere instead of only in a long convoluted circle.

"What?" I yelled over to Leon. "What'd you say?" But it was clear from his face what he'd said. I screeched to a halt and reached over to open his door. He threw up on the running board, on the side of the seat, on his own tuxedo leg, on the pavement. In sight of the Gypsies, whose faces, once the crows cleared, were set like so many frozen white masks in my direction.

We got the hell out of there.

Back at home my father's partner, Mr. Payton, was having a fit. He wanted to leave and I had his car key.

"Where have you been?" my father said. He never really got furious with us. He was too tired. He let my mother handle fury.

"Leon wasn't feeling well. We went on a walk," I said. Leon, to his credit, looked terrible. He had bags under his eyes like bruises. Plus, I'd made him drink from the backyard hose before we went in and his tie was soaked.

"Mr. Payton would like his car," my father said.

Mr. Payton shook. Spit flew when he spoke. "Where've you put it? I was ready to leave fifteen minutes ago." For a moment I could only be amazed at how angry he was.

"We have a party," his wife said. She actually used a cigarette holder.

I volunteered to get the car, but Mr. Payton stuck his hand in my face. "Give me the key, boy." And when I'd pulled it from the tangle of other keys, he added, "I hope you remembered to lock the doors."

"What an ass," I said to my father as we watched them walk down the street, Mr. Payton still ranting.

"A real ass," Leon amended.

"Boys," my father said to us, as if to preamble a long speech, but then didn't go on. He rubbed his cummerbund, soothing his ulcers.

From nowhere, my mother appeared. "Gifts are being opened in there. I expect you'll want to see what they get?" She didn't wait for an answer. This was how she ordered us around.

But we went in. Leon in particular wanted to see how Yvonne liked her gift from him. The first time around, he'd given her wine glasses, all of which had been shattered during one of her fights with Mark.

"I like it," Yvonne said, holding up the Swiss Army knife.

Leon beamed. "It has a plastic toothpick," he told her. To me, it seemed a more dangerous present than the wine glasses.

They got crock pots and coasters and wall-hangings and pot holders and towels and bottles of wine. The best gift was from my Uncle Cy, a fifty-pound fruit basket he'd made himself, packed with everything that would qualify. Sitting on the table, it was taller than Yvonne. To keep the fruit upright, it was wrapped in plastic and tied with a red bow. Pineapple leaves sprouted from the top like a palm tree.

The real action of the day, the event no one would forget, I missed because I stole that fruit basket. While pretending to take all the gifts to Yvonne's room upstairs, I smuggled the fruit basket out the side door. It really did weigh fifty pounds, and I couldn't see over it as I tottered down the block.

The Gypsies' house was also lighted, though not with white light, like ours, but in a sort of murky orange light, like old streetlights. For once, none of them was outside. I had imagined simply setting the basket down at the grandfather's feet, bowing or something in sympathy, and then scurrying off. I could have left the basket on the doorstep, rung the bell, and run, but somehow it didn't seem the right gesture on the night of a funeral.

The one blond child in the family opened the front door. Her skull was too small for her eyes, which bugged out even farther when she saw the fruit. I was struck with momentary dumbness. I had no etiquette to fall back on; I'd never made a sympathy call before.

"Come in," someone said, from a hall door. I stepped in. Their house had a floor plan similar to ours, something you wouldn't have guessed from the outside. The foyer, like ours, had doors leading to all the other rooms of the downstairs, with a stairway at the end.

"I've brought fruit," I said, unnecessary as that was.

"Thank you," the voice said. "Mimi, help him set down his fruit." The little girl led me to a white sideboard and patted its top. I set the basket down and looked at it, completely embarrassed. It was really such a monstrosity.

"I'm sorry," I said, hoping the apology covered everything—

their loss (whoever it was), our family's not inviting the Gypsies to the wedding, my new brother-in-law's behavior, Leon's puking at the gravesite, my ugly gift—but the more I thought about it, the less likely it seemed. Outside, tires screamed around the corner. Of course, that would be one of *our* guests.

The voice, which I thought belonged to the grandfather, but which I now saw belonged to one of the younger men, again said, "Thank you." He stood with his arms crossed over his suit, his eyes burning dark holes in my chest. Even Mimi had retreated from my side and stood behind him. I backed out their front door, sweating in my monkey suit, glad to be outside.

Down the block, hysteria had broken out. People were running in and out, joining and leaving a clump of others on the lawn. Our front door slammed open and shut. I thought rice-throwing must be going on, some last-minute crying and hugging, but when I approached the clump broke open and there was Chris on the lawn, face and suit black with blood. I thought, *The Gypsies have killed my brother-in-law.*

He got shot in the head. Grazed, I guess you'd say. We couldn't call the police. Before he passed out, he'd made that clear, grabbing at Yvonne's dress with his bloody hands. They were not to find out. "I used to know him," he told Yvonne of the gunman, smiling like it was some kid from his first-grade class he'd just met again. Chris's guests, relatives and others, had already begun making preparations, phoning a private ambulance, phoning a private hospital. The private doctor, it turned out, was already among us, attending the wedding. My sister's second wedding ended with her husband being driven to the hospital. Yvonne couldn't even go with him. She would be called.

His guests left soon after, thanking my father for the party.

The women, including my mother, Yvonne, Gerita, the harp-ist, and the roommates, were upstairs. We men took the front stoop.

"Is it Gotto?" my Uncle Cy asked. "Gotto or Gambolini or something like that? Was Chris one of them?"

"Maybe he wasn't but he wanted to be," Leon said. "I was thinking they had to shoot at him to initiate him."

"Who knows? What if they missed and killed him instead? I never heard of such a thing, but who the hell knows?" Cy leaned back on his elbows. "I was beginning to like him," he said. "He was a snook but I liked him anyway."

"That's the past tense," Leon pointed out.

"So it is," Cy said, nodding. He'd pulled off his suspenders and unbuttoned the top button of his pants. Men in our family develop a certain sagginess in their old age.

My father watched the street and I took my cue from him. What was there? Our neighbors' new cyclone fence, ugly enough on its own, but now made uglier by a threatening sign from the sheriff's department on the gate. I could almost read the words from where we sat. They'd been among the first to leave after the shooting, though I knew they were peeking out from their curtains to keep posted. Or maybe my father was remembering when we were all little children, three boys and a girl, a brown-haired, shy, sensitive girl who never seemed to be the one who'd cause trouble. I tried to imagine what worries must be specific to fathers concerning daughters, but how could I?

I said, "Yvonne says you have to change your life every now and then."

"Yeah?" Cy said. "Yeah?" He appeared to think about it. "Hunh," he said. "Today must count for something."

"Yvonne has been reincarnated as a lunatic," Leon said.

But my father said nothing. He wiped his hand through his

slick, thin hair. I thought through all the parts of his life I knew about: my mother, his business partner Mr. Payton, my brother Milo in California, now Yvonne's new husband, Yvonne herself. It suddenly seemed to me, sitting there next to him, that I *was* him, I was my father and his life was happening to me, sitting on my house's front stoop, defeated. I was a man who'd somehow ended up here, married to a woman I no longer felt sparks with, working with a man I couldn't trust, ashamed for having lost my oldest son, so weak as to have allowed my daughter her foolish marriage, looking out at a neighborhood gone not bad, but askew, with cyclone fences and Gypsies and shootings at weddings.

"How does she propose to do such a thing?" my father said. "How does she exactly change her life?" He was tired and sad and beaten. Yes, I thought, tired and sad and beaten myself, how does this miracle come about?

When there wasn't anything left of the evening, when we'd made as much sense of the senseless as we could, we left the scene of today's crime, the bloodstained patch of dirt by the front walk, the plastic champagne glasses upended like futuristic mushrooms grown out of some futuristic mulchy rain, the hulking shadow of the pink Gypsy house on the corner— we left it and entered our well-lit house, where soon we would be joined by the women. By then, my father would be his unfathomable self once again and I would be me, sent to retrieve my Cousin Gerita's Spitfire.

Helen in Hollywood

It was 3:00 A.M. She couldn't sleep. In the distance coyotes yelped bloody murder. Garbage collection would begin soon, sprinklers flush into life, jets roar over so close that the eucalyptus, palm, bougainvillea would shimmer. The world would spring up once more, ducks in a shooting gallery, but for now there were wild coyotes. Only coyotes. Hollywood.

Helen lay in bed trying to remain limp, relaxing her toes, her ankles, knees, thighs, navel, breasts, hands, cheeks. But by the time her eyebrows were tensionless, her toes had curled into anxiety again. She wanted a drink. Digitally, it was 3:45. Symmetry, Helen thought. Whenever she looked at a clock, time was orderly. 1:23. 12:34. 1:11. Without checking the clock, without switching on a lamp, she got up. Flagging her cellular phone was a small yellow Post-it note on which a nameless number had been carefully printed. Helen, cigarette in hand, read over the number and tried to think of ways to remember it. Pneumatic device? she thought, nomadic? Betty, this number belonged to, Betty in Laguna. If only *she*, Helen, had a beach. No wonder Betty hadn't had a drink in six months, had never backslid—her house was on the beach, she'd told them, she sometimes walked straight into the surf when she felt like drinking, diamonds, furs, whatever and all, straight into the waves.

Helen thought of Betty's beach, of ice cubes, of scotch neat, and dialed her number, which she had memorized like so: 72

was high school graduation, 7 years of therapy, 4 people who had ever counted, 38 was how old she'd be when she promised herself she'd be happy, and 6 she just remembered. Six. Betty hadn't had a drink in six months. Betty's phone had rung a good six times before Betty's husband barked into the receiver. Helen listened through the line for waves on Betty's beach until Betty's husband hung up.

In the open refrigerator's light, Helen thought of her ex-husband's house, food stored as if against threat of holocaust. The cleanliness and barrenness of her own refrigerator made her lonely: she was as transient as she felt, it said to her. There was nothing beautiful about her little town house, nothing really of her own making. Sectional furniture, matching appliances, Levolors and track lighting. One million just like it all over L.A., one million more or less similar inhabitants. She missed, suddenly and with acute nostalgia, a purely unique easy chair she'd had when married. She had re-covered it herself, using furry brown-and-white splotched material. The raccoon, they'd named it. But she was not sentimental, as a rule, and she willed the image of the chair to dissipate like so much smoke. Room to room she went, phone in hand. She expected it to ring. Betty would call.

Helen circled the floor plan two or three more times before returning to the living room. Action, she thought. She had to do something, so she began pulling the sectional furniture into separate pieces, then gathering them into a circle. She added one kitchen stool for height. Holding an unsteady flame under another cigarette, she stood in the center of the circle deciding where to sit. She chose a plush, ribbed, bourbon-colored piece of sofa facing a champagne-white wall and cleared her throat.

"It's four in the morning," she said, rustily. "Too late for a decent human to call somebody. Wait, wait." She waved her cigarette before her, eraser style. "I forgot. Hi. My name is Helen. I'm an addict."

She looked around the furniture, then at the framed poster centered by invisible means on the wall. Too many invisible means, Helen thought. Freeways, elevators, television, explosives. The poster commemorated an art show in New York she had not attended, its artist unknown to her. A floating, ephemeral red volcano, green mellifluous smoke, yellow trees swaying dreamily in the foreground. It should have been titled "Napalm" or "Apocalypse."

"Let's don't pretend," she sighed. "If I weren't so lazy and chickenshit, I'd just go buy a bottle and a gun and get it over with."

She sat thoughtfully, listening to the silent plethora of voices raised against this suggestion, a tidal wave rushing a small vessel. "Okay, okay," she said, as if preluding something, then, weakly, "Okay. Let me tell you what happened to me today. I didn't run into any old lovers or my ex-husband. No grade-school teachers, no calls from Mom and Dad. No strange guy who claims I fucked him silly some night three years ago after meeting in a bar in Pasadena, he can remember what sexy dress I wore, what witty comment I made, what damned drink I was drinking. None of that. A basically busy kind of California freeway day. Drive around buying little natural stuff I think I might need. New sheets, all cotton. New seltzer, no salt, no sugar, nothing lethal, plenty of flavor. Right, right. Cigarettes. Think about hiring a hypnotist to stop smoking. Think about buying generic smokes since they taste like burning wheat germ. Think about this funny guy I used to know who taught a snake to smoke. Freak out when I can't remember his name. Practically back-end the onion truck in front of me. Start thinking about that old guy at a meeting who was doing fine, great, Mr. Exemplary until he couldn't remember his mother's maiden name one day and went out to have a drink. 'One shot of tequila,' he tells us, 'and I said, Baliano, that's her name. Just like that.' He was an immigrant, cut necktie linings for a living. Can't remember his mother's maiden name and flips."

Helen stubbed out her cigarette on a drink coaster from La Brea, felt the plastic grow pliant under the butt's heat, and looked at the unyielding empty chairs around her. She sat for a moment trying to think how to go on about the day. Finally she simply moved to the next piece of furniture, which was exactly like the one she'd been on except it had a single plush ribbed arm and cool unflattened nap.

Her view now was of the open partition between living room and kitchen. A ficus rose spinsterlike beside one bar stool. "Hi," she said. "My name's Helen. I'm an addict. You could say I'm addicted to everything bad and nothing good. You have two brothers, say, and the first one is this handsome, clean-cut guy with a 4.0 standing at Harvard Law. He loves me, wants to father a brood of babies who look just precisely like me, set me up in a mansion, hire a vanful of help to do my bidding, finance my dream business. Orchids? Fortune cookie factory? Whatever, and not just money. He loves my soul. Then brother number two. Señor Black Sheep, the guy with the anti-Midas touch—it all goes to ash as soon as he lays his hands on it. Unlucky *and* mean. Evil incarnate. Think of the worst things ever done, here's the guy. If he were smarter, he'd have split the atom. Dumber, he'd be Sirhan Sirhan. But this guy's in between—hunts endangered species, cheats his taxes, cheats his friends, buys love.

"Oh, you can guess the rest. I fall for bachelor number two, every, count them, every time. Well, except one. Mind if I smoke? But it's not just men. I have, bless my soul, all the addictions. Food, drink, dope. Name the poison. It's like I was born without the little switch in your throat, I think it is, that little switch that says enough is enough. Thyroid? Pancreas? Or a brain that just refuses to admit the word *moderation*. Permanent block. 'Just one drink? Only eight ounces of ice cream, not the whole gallon? A husband but no boyfriends? No way. Does not compute.' " Helen suddenly smacked herself on the cheek, one and then the other, matter of fact and without a flinch. Afterwards, she slid to another seat.

"Hi my name is Helen I'm an addict," she said. "So what else is new? I want to tell you about the perfect day in my life. I had one several years ago and I swear it ruined the rest. You read about young brilliant people? Write a million-dollar novel or a symphony or break a genetic code when they're still like ten or something? But think: what can ever happen to them except to fizzle? They're going to kill themselves, right? Someday they're going to see they topped out before puberty and the rest's a downhill plunge. Hey, you live in Hollywood you've got to believe it. Okay, so that's how this one day was, for me. It couldn't have been better and no other day will ever even be in the race. Why go on? I won't get suicidal on you, I just want to pose the philosophical question, why go on when you've apexed?

"Let me set the scene: I've been married one year. All the kinks are worked out. We know each other's buttons, but we aren't pushing them yet. We're in the middle of the New Mexico desert at sunset. Not a single other vehicle. World's annihilated and John and I are what's left and we just saw a coyote, I swear, chasing a roadrunner. Laugh ourselves hysterical. Everything is like laundry hanging on a line. Dry, stiff, clean. It has been unrelentingly, hellishly hot all day, but now has cooled just enough—the air is sweet to the touch. Cotton candy, melts on your tongue. We stop to stretch, to watch the sky crescendo, and when I lift my arms I feel like the sun might just evaporate me up whole in purple and red and orange. It's like sex in heaven. It really could be the end of the world, we say, nuclear Fourth of July. We're on our way home from visiting his parents. His father's dying. Also an addict, cigarettes, booze. Still hits it hard, after about a hundred strokes. Can hardly talk, hardly change a TV channel, but smoking and drinking like a house on fire.

"Cheerful? Well, no, but understand, we were out of there. We'd paid a visit, a last visit, we thought—although it turned out later he lived forever and ever, longer than the wife—and had done all we could do. He was self-destructive, we told ourselves, happy as clams. We'd gone to show support for the wife, to pay respects. Okay, to feel better about ourselves. See? It worked. I was ecstatic, giddy, from so much self-congratulation. We were gone, clean getaway, en route to our not unpleasant life. Our problems? Small and far away, like death. We were on the desert, halfway home. He wanted to make love, crush into the backseat like teenagers. He grabbed my ass and pulled me to him. I loved my husband. Without reservation, for that day. I thought if I could simply keep the balance I suddenly, for the first time, felt, then I could always be happy, just like then. I thought, 'So this is the recipe for a good life. You throw in equal parts beauty, self-delusion, smugness, optimism, and distant despair. Voilà—a sunset to please even an unsentimental God.' Ludicrous, of course. A week later and I bottomed out. You don't want to hear about it. Actually, truthfully, you didn't want to hear the good part, 'fess up. You people would rather hear about when I sank. I won't give you the satisfaction." Helen crossed her legs. "Fuck you all very much."

She got up and went to the bedroom again. 4:44. In a spurt of meaningful activity, she pulled off her Lakers T-shirt and flowered leggings and got dressed quickly. Bra, panties, jeans, flip-flops. She yanked drawers open in search of the right shirt, finally settling on the one she'd just taken off. In the bathroom, she moussed her fingers and worked them through her flat perm, pulling it into shape. Afterwards she splashed her face and rubbed gel rouge on both cheeks, then spread some on her mouth for good measure.

She blinked at her reflection, licking her lips and tasting the rouge. "Hell," she watched her reflection enunciate. Not enough laugh lines, receding gums. "Goddamn hell. Hi, my name is Helen. I'm an addict." She lowered herself to the tub's rim. "Hi, my name is Helen Elizabeth Dugas Walcott, I'm an addict. I wish I could tell you some interesting trauma of my life. I wish I could just produce anecdote upon anecdote, like that Korean prostitute from Seattle. Remember her? One jaded saga after another, nonstop. Father drove an ambulance, mother ran an underground railway, this girl escapes Korea by marrying an ambassador's son, who rapes her to prove he can fuck women. Dumps her in New York City. She hooks her way west. Tragic, but she was so funny. And here I am, unable to dredge up even one subconscious atrocity. I was loved as a kid, un-abused, my parents had another child, basically, to give me a friend. I did well in school, I married a great guy who I turned into a demon. The rest of you have legitimate reasons for being here, but I can't think what mine might be. I'm self-indulgent and ungenerous and lazy. I wish you'd all give me a spanking and then electrocute me. I'll just fill this here tub, sit down, and you guys toss in the toaster."

Dressed, Helen wandered back into the kitchen and almost opened the refrigerator again, but instead checked the supply of staples in their canisters. "Biscuits," she said hopefully. But there was no milk. This reminded her of something from college, so she returned once more to the circle.

"I was bulimic. I cured that on my own because I used to have willpower, which I guess just went out the window somewhere along the line. Oh yeah. Hi my name is Helen I'm an addict. Anyway, I was this very scientific bulimic. My meals were planned for easy vomiting. It's nauseating, tell me about it, but when you're being honest, what's not? Life is sickening, just accept it. You want a pretty picture, buy a postcard.

"Okay, first you eat something sort of light and airy, like caramel corn or scrambled eggs or ice cream. That provides a coating on the bottom. Next, eat your meal. Roast beef, potatoes, cooked carrots. Biscuits. Just be sure to take little sips of milk every few bites. You have to have liquid, but not too much liquid. Too much liquid and you never get that food back up. Too little and it's very hard work. After the meal, dessert, of course, then more dessert, then maybe a peanut butter and jelly sandwich. Pizza. What you put on as topping can be anything—heavy stuff, lumpy stuff, even a candy bar. No liquid at this point. No no no. Wait approximately half an hour. Find an unpopulated bathroom. You know the rest. Afterwards drink plenty of water right away; otherwise, you get light-headed, shaky. Brush your teeth. Re-apply makeup. Sit by yourself for a few minutes to let your face recover its normal pallor. Simple, huh? Do this three times a day for six years. Get pretty tired of it, worried about it, then cut back. Promise yourself only two vomits a day, then one, except for weekends, et cetera. Finally, quit cold turkey. How do you think I *knew* I couldn't be moderate with everything else in my life? However, I *did* kick food."

Helen lit her fourth cigarette and then reached over her shoulder to pat herself. She left her hand there for a moment, a half hug, then abruptly shrugged it off and changed seats. Before her now was a shelf of books, their covers the eye-catching colors of fast-food chains. Self-help books, Helen thought, literary burger and fries. It occurred to her that the only good thing about them was also the only good thing about meetings: someone somewhere was worse off. Really, Helen had lost the ability to be alarmed. Stories of ruined lives rolled over her without leaving the faintest impression. That in itself could be considered alarming, she decided.

"It's a sad state of affairs," she said from her new seat, "when four persons constitute the real world—that's Real World in caps. They aren't anybody's four persons but mine. Yes, they're all mine. Number one, Natalie Bennett, the sorriest saddest woman I ever knew, landlady and chiseler and gossip and self-righteous moralizer. Another God-aholic. A woman wrong in all her parts. I swear, the one person whose life I wouldn't inhabit for all the money and pleasure in the world. Her ugliness keeps me in the halo's light, if you see what I mean. The grass on her side of the fence is tundra.

"Number two, my ex, John. We're all well acquainted with John. I loved him, and then I didn't. It's not like there weren't warnings early on. After we'd been married, say six hours, I woke up and saw that gold band on my finger and thought about the best man. It's an old story, right? You get what you want, you don't want it. For a while I wished he would die. Simple. No responsibility on my part. He dies in a wreck, plane or car, who cares? I am the widow, sad but free. The best man comes to the funeral—think: best man and pallbearer, all in one year. He stays with me. We come together in shared grief, our love growing between us as if *he* were still there to bond us . . .

"But John survives. Survives and survives. Five married years he survives. We have a son. I love John for the son. How can I help it? He looks like his father, he loves us together, he loves to lie between us on the bed and stretch his little hands to feel both parents at once. We are all naked, or nearly, and I see the world differently. Parents, children, nakedness. Simple, like love.

"And John loves me. Can you possibly know how his love kills me? Moony eyes, pathetic little embraces. He wants to make love. He wants to make love. I feign sleep, disinterest, listen to him as he goes at it on his own beside me. He's a good man. He's willing to do, believe me, anything. Anything I say. What power. What prison. Yes, there are moments, I told you, I concede, goddammit, when I come close to loving him, to loving us. When he holds that sleeping boy and strokes his hair, looking to me to thank me, to feel that we are blessed, lucky, and if I can muster affection, gratitude, even for only that moment, then that is as near as I pass, I swear, to love."

Helen sighed. She said, "Number three, my son John Junior. I can't talk about John Junior. These meetings don't seem to leave room for talking about some things, believe it or not, and one of them is Johnny. You can imagine. Sure you can. We were in the paper. Were we in the paper? If only you could child-proof a mother the way you can a kitchen—safety latches, outlet covers, unscrewable lids. I'll just tell you about number four, the retarded guy who opens the gate at the plastics factory in Lawrence, Kansas, who could explain in alarming detail at four in the morning the workings of plastic margarine-tub making, the de-construction, instrument by instrument, of an untranscribed version of 'But Not for Me,' which I seemed to be humming. The idiot savant, the kindest human who ever was, the man who brought me a hunting jacket, cup of decaf, and who shared his black boxed lunch after witnessing a single car accident involving, natch, my automobile. An accident of which I have no memory. I'd been in Kansas City; suddenly I saw Mortland Cryer, his name badge upside down, peering in my windshield, wondering aloud if I was a dead lady."

Helen sat on her hands and then lifted herself and teetered for a moment. "Old Mortland Cryer is the antidote to Natalie Bennett, see what I mean? They're the two sides of that scale. And here's me, in the middle, Ms. Justice herself. At least I'm not Natalie Bennett, I think. I'm not Mortland Cryer either, but someone like Mortland Cryer is out there functioning, opening his gate, assisting delinquents like me along in life. And John and John. On a good day they're—yes, yes, I admit it—my higher beings. On a bad one? Albatross. The thing is, these four people live in me like a disease. In remission, then not. One minute they make me want to dance, the next I feel like self-immolating. You know what I mean?"

When she moved, she sat tipped forward, grinning. "Next? Doesn't anyone else have something to share? Helen's been very open with us all, and I think she deserves a hand." Helen clapped, smiling cheerily, leaning toward a piece of the sectional couch across from her as if congratulating its occupant. "How about you, Helen?" she said to the kitchen stool. "How's tricks?" She immediately jumped up and took the stool, slouching on it, assuming a belligerent posture.

"Nah, don't bug me," she said. "I just came to listen today. These meetings are starting to get to me. I dream about them. My dreams are full of people who beat themselves up, red eyes, scarred wrists, DT's, diminished capabilities. Over-this, over-that, men, women, adult children. Really, it's more like the group disease, the compulsion to blab and blab and *blab*. Sometimes I think you people are addicted to each other. Twelve steps? Please. It's the new religion, except now there's twelve steps instead of ten commandments. Always the higher power. No, no, no, Helen, you are not responsible.

You're only as sick as your secrets. Don't believe in God? *No hay problema.* Remember the woman and her Samoyed? One more Saturday morning listening to that woman revere her fucking dog." Helen shook the memory the way she might shake off an insect, and scooted back to her former seat.

"Hmm. You're feeling anger, Helen. Anyone want to talk with Helen about this?"

Back on the kitchen stool, Helen looked around, daring a response. "I'd just like to say one thing," she said, moving left into another, softer chair. "I'd just like to say that I'm in agreement with Helen here. Most of you are total bunk. Excuse me, but it's true. Get a good night's sleep and your problems are gone. Me, for instance. I just want to sleep. More than anything. Wake up tomorrow in the sunshine. Go to Betty's beach, lie naked in the sun, sleep like the dead. You think I love sex best? Pills? Booze? Boys? Wrong. Sunshine on my skin. Lying on the beach listening to the waves. Nature's narcotic. One baptismal wash after another, whoosh. Whoosh." She paused, hands poised before her, open, then clenching air as they fell like a wave. "Whoosh." Another moment. "Whoosh. And the sun just shines. Bodies love the sun. I don't care about this melomania or whatever. Your skin can tell you. It's a sun junky. Just ask."

Helen lay back on her seat and pulled her feet underneath her. Exhausted but not anywhere near sleep, she reached behind her for the hanging plastic stick that opened the Levolors. "I'm betting," she said, twisting the octagonal stick in her fingers, "that the sun's rising even now, while we speak. Takers?" Through the open blinds oblique, questionable light fell in lines on the circle of chairs. At Helen's feet, the phone shrilled, once, twice, and from the bedroom came the toneless humming buzz of her digital alarm. It was 5:55 and time to get up.

You Boys Be Good

I'm at Uncle Guy's, playing gin rummy. He wins most hands, I win some. We play for pennies, and later, when the game gets going, buttons out of my Aunt Cy's sewing basket. She went off in her car—where, Guy and I both cannot remember. He thought it was the grocery store; I thought it was Miss Head's place. All she said was "You boys be good." We can't agree on what Cy wore when she left the house either, though we think, after a while, that it probably had some blue in it, whatever it was. We remembered a bit of blue flashing by when she left.

The important thing, Guy says, is that she's gone. "I love her," he says, often, actually. "But I also love smoked almonds," and then he pushes away the carrot sticks Cy left for us and gets the almonds out of their hiding place. "Just have to remain calm while I'm eating them," he says. "That's the secret to high blood pressure."

He is my great-uncle by marriage, hardly related at all, and he looks just like the sort of man who gets high blood pressure, so that's no surprise. He's seventy-three, heavy, bald, and has a hook nose covered with broken blood vessels. He wears glasses so thick that when he looks up at me, over his cards, his eyes are raw eggs. "Gin!" he says, flapping down his straight, bouncing a little in his chair, and then he tells himself to relax, calm down. He shuts his eyes and puts both hands on the table, like he's keeping it grounded, and says,

"RELAX," three times, an incantation. When he opens his eyes, he smiles at me and writes down his score. "Heh heh," he says, and I shuffle and deal like a good loser. He's the one person I don't mind losing to.

Guy is not a good loser. I try to gin very quietly when I do happen to win. We both approach my winning as carefully as possible. Sometimes I even shuffle and deal for him. Meanwhile, Guy eats nut after nut, popping them into his mouth with two hands, shifting in his chair, more like a monkey than a man. Inside, I'm sure he's telling himself to relax, relax.

This is what I won't do: I won't *let* him win; he has to win fair.

Every Friday night goes like this. Cy leaves to shop or visit, and we play cards. I live in their garage, surrounded by barber chairs and boxes of linen towels, leftovers from Guy's business. I sit in the chairs to read or just spin around. Cy comes out to visit now and then, but mostly they leave me alone. They probably think I'm making big decisions about life. Guy never asks me why don't I have a date on Friday night—he just assumes I'd rather be playing cards here, which maybe is true.

"That Cy?" he says. A car crunches through the gravel alley.

"She's at Miss Head's," I say. Every week we go through this. Guy worries, I reassure.

"Or the grocery," Guy says. "She went to Miss Head's last week." But he looks to me to confirm this, he can't really remember. Sometimes he forgets my name and calls me Bill Willy, nobody I've even heard of. Sometimes he starts saving cards for the last hand he had instead of the one he's holding. If Cy's gone and I'm not here either, he can lose years of his life, suddenly think he's still running the barber shop and is late for an appointment, some half-wit trainee cutting an important customer's hair. It's a little frightening, a little funny.

Guy leans forward in his chair, straddling it, tapping his foot. He looks like a baseball catcher, somebody who might have been athletic. He covers his bald head with his free hand, and it occurs to me that I wouldn't trust a bald barber. I tell him this and he laughs until tears form. Then he gins.

"Mother of pearl!" he says, grinning. Another car makes a noise outside and he grabs the almonds, ready to hide them again. The car passes. He points to me. "You're in charge of the nuts. They're making me crazy."

Tonight we play to five hundred, our usual number. Guy keeps score on a flowered bridge pad, one of Cy's from bridge club. He writes so hard the score is pressed into the rest of the pad. The pencil lead breaks and surprises him. He sharpens it with his pocketknife. It's this moment, or sooner, that Cy usually comes home.

"Cy should be coming, right?" He looks at the clock on the wall, tries to read my watch. I put away the almonds. He sorts the cards into suits. He asks me if I've found a girl to fall in love with. I tell him not yet. He says not to marry anybody whose name rhymes with mine, that's a bad joke that no one ever lets up on.

"No problem," I say. "I can't think of a single name that rhymes with Paul."

"Saul," he says. "Polly, Molly, Jolly. I never knew anyone named Polly. What a shame." He pulls the cards back out of the pack and starts shuffling, but then puts them away again. "Where's Cy?" he asks me. "I think she's late."

"I'll stay till she gets here," I say, but this isn't what he's worried about because his face doesn't relax, though he tells it to. "She's probably watching a show at Miss Head's," I say, "and she doesn't want to miss the end. She wants to know who the murderer is."

He nods. "That Cy likes to have all the answers. All the answers."

"We could call Miss Head's," I say. But Guy shakes his head, no, emphatically. He looks disappointed in me for even suggesting such a thing. We can't check up on Cy.

So we sit and listen to cars for a while. Then Guy puts his big hand over mine and says, "Let's look at the atlas!" This is the road atlas, the maps of all the states, also Canada and Mexico. Guy likes to plan trips he can't take. For one thing, there's his weak heart, the blood pressure. For another thing, Cy has her shut-ins to visit. Guy and I have a sketchy plan to drive around Oklahoma in the summer, visit people he's barely related to, check in on his father's grave, see how the cemetery's doing.

His atlas is so old the interstate doesn't exist. The states are free of highway lines and look as if the huge prairies are still there. He turns to Kansas and traces the tornado belt across the center, jabs at Liberal, where his sister Vileen has a trailer park. He is absorbed in marking with his pencil all the places he's visited, an X for having spent the night, an O for just driving through.

"Now what time is it?" he asks me as I'm checking it myself.

"Ten o'clock," I say, though it's a few minutes past.

"Cy hates the news show," Guy says. "She wouldn't watch that." There hasn't been a car making any noise anywhere for the last half hour. "So she should be home," he explains. We watch the minute hand go around on the wall clock.

"Here we are in Lawton," I say, pointing to us on the map. "You want to go to Tulsa?"

"Ponca City," he says. He bends back over the map, draws a

hard line with his pencil from Lawton to Ponca City, then makes an *X*. "We'll stay overnight in the motel." He turns to me. "Unless you know somebody there?"

"No one," I say.

A car finally goes by outside; Guy lets out his breath like he's been holding it for hours. "Where *is* she?" he says, and I hear his worry take a turn toward anger. "Relax," he reminds himself, wiping the sweat from his head. "Relax." He takes his glasses off, which makes his eyes seem to shrink into his face, as if he's been exposed to bright light. They become strangely birdlike. "Let's have a *vodka*," he whispers, squinting so his eyes become smaller yet.

Vodka, of course, is much worse than smoked almonds. It must seem to him, as it does to me, that Cy would *have* to come home if we got out the vodka. So we head for the basement, where the vodka's hidden. We take two small glasses, a lime, and the atlas. Guy laughs a nervous laugh when he pours our drinks. "To Cy," he says, and we toast. We down our drinks and wait to hear her drive up. Nothing. We wait some more.

"You like vodka?" he says to me, and I tell him it's pretty good. "The best!" he says. "Let's have another, just a little." He cuts himself with his pocketknife slicing the lime. "Don't bleed in the drinks," he says to his thumb.

"To Cy," I say, holding up my glass, "who's on her way home," and when I say it, I know it's true. She'll be here soon.

"To Cy," Guy says, blinking behind his glasses. His watery eyes focus on mine as sharply as they can for a second, as if he sees into my skull and is surprised at what's there. "She's the best redhead in the world," he says suddenly. And then he spills his vodka on the atlas. He grabs my arm, makes me spill mine.

"She's okay, Guy. She'll be here," I say, convinced. He waves that away, doesn't say anything. "Vodka's all right, once in a while," I say. Still he doesn't speak, stands looking at his wet atlas. The pencil lines widen and fade under the vodka.

"I didn't know Cy had red hair," I say.

"It was red," Guy says, still looking down, "before it was gray. Listen, Bill Willy . . ." His voice changes tones, is directed at the floor. "Sometimes," he says, cocking his head, "I *think* the wrong things."

"Guy," I say.

"Thinking's bad," he says, "but *saying*'s worse." He puts his hand back on my wrist, doesn't look up. "There's this story about a man who had a wife and she went out one night and didn't come home for a long time." He takes a breath, seems to wait for me to respond.

"With another man?" I say softly. I try hard to picture Cy with some man.

"No, no, no." He shakes his head impatiently. "Not like that. Mother of *pearl*. The wife was in an *accident*. A car accident. The husband waited and waited and then the neighbors called to tell him because in the wife's pocketbook it said to call the neighbors instead of the husband in emergency situations." He stops. I don't know if he's concerned with the accident part or the calling the neighbors part. Maybe both.

"Cy wasn't in an accident," I finally say. "She's just late. Not even very late." I try to show him the time on my watch, but the basement's dim.

"Well, they took this lady to the hospital," Guy says, "and they operated right away, there was glass in her everywhere." He stops again to catch his breath, to put his hand against the basement wall. "But she died." We are quiet. I listen for sirens in the night, don't hear a thing.

"Did you know this man?" I say, looking for where this fits, what's important. "Did you know them?"

"And after she died," Guy says, pressing on the wall, "the doctor gave the husband her things, on the same night it happened, you see. Her personal effects. Her rings, her necklace, her purse, her watch." He stops and looks at my watch. "Her wig."

"Her wig?"

"And there was blood on it. And vomit. She was a redhead and they gave her husband her hair. Do you understand?"

I shake my head. I can't even imagine.

"The husband said . . ." He stops, looks confused. "I think I must have read this in a newspaper," he says, "I kind of remember *print*. Anyway, the husband said, 'I never knew, I never knew.' He was talking about the *hair*. He never knew it was a wig." Guy peers at me.

"But you know Cy better than that?" I guess. "You know hair better than that?"

"When I read about it, I was pretty young. We lived in Blackman." He points with his finger to southern Oklahoma. "Do you know what I thought, though? The very first thing that popped into my head? This: why would anyone *choose* to have red hair? And worse than that, the worst thing in the *world*," he whispers to me, coming closer, "I *said* it to Cy, sitting at breakfast, just off the top of my head." He touches his head briefly, indicating the top of it.

"Let's go back upstairs," I say. His story has made me edgy.

"There she was with red hair," Guy says to himself, wagging his head, "right at breakfast." He holds my arm going up the steps. His fingers are like ice. We leave the glasses and atlas in the basement, so when we turn off the light and shut the basement door the whole scene disappears. Once we're in the kitchen again, it would be a good time for Cy to show up, but she doesn't.

Guy sits without straddling his regular chair and takes off

his glasses. He rubs his eyes, hard, and says, "I remember what Cy was wearing when she left. It was her green muumuu. No blue whatsoever. What do you think?"

"Sounds good," I say, though at this moment I can't recall any detail of Cy. All I see when I close my eyes is a redheaded wig with blood and vomit. Did the husband think of it as *her*? It might have seemed alive. But why didn't he know she wore a wig? I can't even decide which question is the important one.

"What are you going to do when Cy gets here?" I ask Guy. "What are you going to say?"

"I'll tell her I won, five hundred to fifty-seven," he says. "I'll ask her if old Miss Head is still alive." He stands up and gets himself a glass of water. "I'll try not to act too surprised when she comes home to me."

Dog Problems

You always heard that dogs could smell fear; this dog could smell love. Whenever people were touching, embracing, kissing, she would be there, offering her front paw or nose for a similar embrace. She horned in on several moments a day. And there were times when David felt she was the most loved of the three of them.

She came into their marriage as more of a nanny, an older, pleasant enough female with a tolerance for interruptions to the schedule. She'd always been allowed to sleep in the bedroom, right next to Adrienne, but David, in their first year of marriage, had felt he wasn't having enough things his way. Not that Blanche bothered him at night—most nights he couldn't have said one way or the other whether she was in the room—but he wanted to be able to choose, and so he chose the backyard.

She went with only the mildest of sighs, aware, David was sure, of her own innocence in the situation. Every night Adrienne stood with her in the yard telling her good night. They'd play a halfhearted game of fetch, both of them conscious that though two had gone out, only one would return to the bedroom. Sometimes, in the black hours of the early morning, Adrienne would suddenly wake and, before David could move, be out the door, her robe swinging around her, worried about Blanche.

His family had had a dog while he was growing up, but he

didn't have very clear memories of it. Sergio, he was named, a big drooling oily kind of dog who spent most of the time digging an enormous tunnel under the toolshed. The backyard stank of him. It was always someone's chore to feed him, a chore that was as odious and regimented as emptying the trash or plunging the bathtub.

On the other hand, Adrienne had gotten Blanche in high school, named her from *Streetcar*, and taken her everywhere. She was a treat, not a chore. In college, Blanche smoked pot, had an ear pierced, sported a Magic Marker Picasso on her broad back. Blanche wore a bandana and rode in the bed of many boyfriends' trucks. She was a pal, a dog everyone loved, a dog who mostly seemed to take care of Adrienne instead of the other way around.

Blanche had meals twice a day, just like Adrienne. Breakfast was dog chow with powdered milk and warm water; dinner, dog chow with bouillon and more warm water. She was eleven years old, her teeth could no longer chew hard food, and the rest of her system wouldn't digest canned. Adrienne mothered her, spoiled her even. Blanche had only to sound a single yip in the morning and Adrienne was out of bed and on her way. David, still foggy with sleep, heard them through the heat vents, the cabinets opening, then shutting, the food rattling into the shallow tin pan that was Blanche's plate, the water running until it matched the temperature of Adrienne's wrist, just like any other child's food. And then Adrienne made her own breakfast, coffee and a heaped spoonful of crunchy peanut butter. After that, they went outside to sit in the sun. Blanche retrieved the newspaper, every day except Sunday, when it was too large for her teeth to hold.

Later, if Adrienne remembered, she would come back to bed for a few moments, roll next to David in her robe, and nudge backwards into his rib cage and stomach. She called it invading the fetus. When they were first married, five years ago, she came back to bed every morning, sometimes more than once, eager for him to wake. Now, she seemed to prefer being alone. Well, not strictly: there was Blanche, of course.

Today, however, Adrienne graced his frontside with her backside, bumping up against his erection with the crease between her buttocks. "Howdy," she said. Then, "Come on, Blanche." The dog heaved herself onto the bed, always careful to stay on Adrienne's side of it, and curled into Adrienne. "Three spoons," Adrienne said, completely happy.

After she had left for work, David called in sick.

"You're not really sick," his partner, Robinson, said. "Not really, right?"

David was annoyed: he would have told Robinson the truth, that he was just down, tired of going to work, feeling a need to remain in his terry-cloth bathrobe—except Robinson tried to outguess him first. Instead, he said, "No, I woke up with the runs. Plus a toothache." Two inconsistent symptoms were better than two normally complementary ones, headache and fever, for example.

"Drag, man."

"Yeah."

"Okay. I'll be at the Stivaks', shoveling rocks, in case you get well later on."

The Stivaks. A whole swimming pool, cabaña, and archaic heat pump to landscape around. Also, the son had allergies. David and Robinson had already had to dig up a Palo Verde tree, its root system some sort of world's record. A kid with allergies had no business in the desert. "Fat chance," David said.

Robinson laughed. "You ain't sick."

"I got the runs, believe me."

"Okay, okay." Robinson would be looking up at the sky, thinking about heat, imagining the day over instead of beginning. "Bye." He said it like a sheep, *bah.*

They hung up. David, free for the day, took a tour of the house. Blanche followed, toenails clicking. She was half golden retriever, half husky, lumpy and round with fur like a bear rug. The white on her muzzle was creeping toward her ears, soon to take over her honey back and tail. She sat down on David's feet at Adrienne's dresser, a small reminder that he was not supposed to be opening Adrienne's little boxes, fingering her trinkets.

Adrienne collected and David threw away. That's how he would have categorized them today, looking at her junk. Though she was twenty-six, the filler in the boxes could have been a high school girl's. It was one notch higher than Cracker Jack fare, one notch lower than valuable. Stuff, and about twenty little boxes full. Everyone in her family was an accessory to this crime; stuff boxes were all they could ever think to give her, every Christmas and birthday rounding up a few more, every vacation they'd send one to her. Hawaii, Fiji, Japan . . . David jumped. Blanche barked out the window at two girls jogging by. They looked toward the noise, and David, without thinking about it, shied behind the curtains: caught at his wife's boxes.

"Hush!"

Blanche pulled her front paws off the windowsill and dropped to her haunches, obedient.

"Shake." She shook.

"Lie down." She lay.

"All the way down." She lowered her chin to the floor, eyes on him.

"Okay, Blanche, here's the clincher: fix me a Denver omelet." She continued watching him, not batting an eyelid, humorless, as David had always contended. They both perked up when they heard the front door open.

"Blanche?" Adrienne shouted. "Hey, Blanche." David considered hiding, spying on the two of them; what was it they did alone, anyway? But it was too late—there was Adrienne at the doorway. She grabbed her throat when she saw him.

"Oh you scared me!" She stepped backwards. "What are you doing here?"

"I called in sick. I got the runs." It was a handy illness, amazingly vivid for being just one word.

She wrinkled her face. "Can I do anything?"

He shrugged. "Just don't feel like working."

She nodded, her heavy breathing moving her chest.

"What are *you* doing here?" he said.

"Well, on the way to the bus I saw this dog, a little black and brown dog, in the street. I mean, there was traffic . . . " She headed toward the kitchen, telling the story over her shoulder. David followed, just like Blanche. Adrienne was in the Tupperware cupboard, rummaging through the lids. ". . . I called to it, but it wouldn't come, so I turned my back and then it came. One of *those* kind of dogs. Not like you, big Blanche." Blanche smiled, flattered.

Adrienne pulled out a custard keeper, then dove back in for its top. "So I had to coax it backwards, you know, pretending I wasn't interested, until it was out of the street. It could have been a stray except it was wearing a collar. But it was *so* thin." She'd uncovered a lid and was now filling the custard keeper with Blanche's dog pellets. Blanche whisked her tail on the floor, licked her chops. "No, baby, not for you." Abruptly the tail stopped. "So I turned around. I thought I would just look in the paper real fast and see if there was a lost-and-found ad, but then, you won't believe this, on the way home I saw a notice on the telephone pole for a little black dog with tan markings. I couldn't believe it." She shook her hair out of her face, snapped the lid on, burped it. "326-0775. I'm going to call. Then I'm going to feed it till whoever owns it gets there. What do you think?"

David blinked into the blank space the end of her story had made. He thought that nothing like that would happen to him on his way to work, that if he saw a dog he wouldn't think twice, but he said, "I think that's a good idea."

Disappointed, mildly disappointed in his answer, but too happy in her busyness to be disappointed for long, she picked up the phone, singing, "Three two six oh seven seven five," and dialed. She hooked the receiver between her shoulder and chin and pulled Blanche to her, ruffling her face. "Oh, come on," she told the phone. Finally, she hung up. She pursed her lips, shook the Tupperware of dog food, and then calmed Blanche, who'd thought she'd seen a second chance at the pellets. "Well, I'll feed it, anyway. And I'll just call later. But what if it goes back in the street? Maybe I should bring it here and put it in the pen. But what if it has rabies?" She worked through these while David watched. "I'll call from work, tell them the dog is in this neighborhood and they can come get it. After all, it's lived this long without my help." Satisfied, she kissed Blanche, then David, took her dog food, and left.

The house was quiet again, nothing to indicate she'd been there at all. David wished he had gone to work. He wished he had volunteered to join her with the stray. He wished he had anything besides watching Donahue to do. It was in this boredom that he decided to give Blanche a bath. She stank, as always, and Adrienne would appreciate it. Besides, bathing her would absolve some of his growing guilt at sticking Robinson with the Stivaks' rocks.

First he took his own shower, before the tub got filthy. Blanche lay on the bathmat, ignorant of what was coming, and tried to lick his legs when he got out. Apparently,

Adrienne allowed this for, try as he might, he'd never been able to break the dog of it. True, her tongue felt nice, soft and caressing, but still, wasn't this how they gave you worms?

"Okay, Blanche. Bath time," he said. She crawled under the sink, trying to get small, trying to become heavier, trying to cling to the tile with her nails. "Out. Now." He pulled and she pulled. He almost gave up, almost felt sorry enough and respectful enough (after all, she was nearly eighty years old) to quit, but Adrienne would love to have her clean, would love him for cleaning her.

"Out!" he said, and yanked her onto the bathmat. He then slid the dog, on the mat, to the tub and hefted her in.

David had had an uncle who lived with David's family for as long as he could remember. Uncle Festes. Infestes, David and his brothers called him. Festes was a cheerful, doddering, mostly harmless alcoholic who took great pains to hide his affliction from the family. They all knew anyway. He would come into the kitchen after a night on the town and say, regretfully, apologetically, shaking his head sorrowfully, "Bottle problems." That was it.

If David's one sister, Leticia, whose job it was to fix breakfast should burn something, which happened frequently, Festes would say, "Toast problems," and shake his head, sadly but without anger. What could you do? he seemed to say. Some nights, because there were too few beds and not nearly enough space to hold them all, they would fight. These were "P.M. problems."

David hadn't thought of his Uncle Festes in a long time. While scrubbing Blanche's hand-sized paws, he thought *dog problems*. Adrienne had gone out and found one, and here he was with his own. It was a good approach, a basically safe one. Shrug your shoulders and take the problem by the hand.

He hadn't dressed after his shower, figuring, correctly, that he would only have to change again after a round with Blanche in the tub. They both rested leaning against the wet porcelain in their respective corners, waiting for the bell that would send them back to the fight. Blanche threatened to shake her wet fur, and David responded by lifting the squeeze bottle of flea shampoo to her nose. There was something satisfyingly masculine about wrestling naked with a wet dog. David could get his teeth into this, he thought. For her part, Blanche kept her tail out of the water, staring straight ahead at the hot and cold faucets and blinking like a tortured prisoner when he rinsed.

David left the bathroom as Blanche stepped out; matron from the tub, she could attend to her drying off by herself. He put his bathrobe back on, beginning to believe he did have the runs. And a toothache, he reminded himself, reaching for his jaw. He mixed a Bloody Mary and opened the bathroom door.

Blanche stood dripping on the bathmat. She hadn't shaken, and that alarmed David. He set down his drink, which then fell over. The glass rolled on the carpet of the hallway, the cubes slid on the tile of the bathroom floor. The Bloody Mary formed a stain. Blanche trembled, then ceased, then trembled again, her eyes at David's waist, not accusing, not forgiving.

"Shake, buddy." David stepped into the humid room and pulled several towels from the racks, draping them over her. She vibrated beneath his palms. Drool formed a long strand from the corner of her mouth to the floor. "Oh, Christ," David said, "oh, Christ. Come on, come on." He decided to take her outside in the sun, warm her up, and dry her off. A bath wouldn't kill her, he told himself, luring her step by wet step through the house and out the back door, a bath wouldn't kill her.

She stood as before, this time on the redwood deck David and Robinson had built in an off-week. Despite the sun, her back and legs quivered, her tail drooped. What had happened in the five minutes it had taken to pull on his robe and mix a drink? "Fuck," he said. "Come on Blanche, pal, shape up." The dog wouldn't even meet his eyes. He would have to call Adrienne. The thought of calling her was worse than the sight of the dog before him, two strands of drool now connecting her with the deck.

He dragged the phone onto the porch and dialed, twice incorrectly. Blanche didn't listen as he told her help was on the way, soon Adrienne would be there. But Adrienne hadn't come in yet; her boss was wondering, herself, where she could be. For a second, David wondered: where was Adrienne anyway? Then he remembered the stray. Then Blanche. He said, "Tell her to call me. It's an emergency at home. Dog problems."

"Oh dear," said her boss. "Not Blanche?"

David resented this: she knew the dog? He'd never even met Adrienne's boss, and yet here she was, familiar with their dog. He wanted to ask if she knew his name as well. "Yeah," he said, "Blanche. Maybe you can tell me what to do. She's all quivery . . . "

"No, no, I don't know a thing about animals. I rely on the veterinarian, I'm afraid."

"Well, tell Adrienne to call."

Blanche had knelt, all four legs buckled, as if suspended in mid-jump. She panted. She looked like she was doing a push-up, like she was a lizard.

At the vet's, a thousand things occurred to him, most of them having to do with Adrienne's blaming him for what had happened to her dog, whatever that would be. The vet, instead of escorting the two of them into a cubicle, had called her assistant and taken Blanche to the back, leaving David in the waiting room, pacing like an expectant father in a B movie.

Now he played out a few scenarios: Blanche died, Adrienne wept and wept and never recovered. David would then discover, as he probably subconsciously had known all along, that she loved the dog more than him. And why not? She'd had her longer, grown up with her, confided to her all her secrets. Another scenario: Blanche died and David disappeared, caught the next train out, leaving the dog corpse with the vet and Adrienne with a mystery.

David stood before a colorful cartoon poster. It told how to brush a dog's teeth, beginning with a paper towel or soft cloth and just rubbing, eventually moving up to toothpaste and a soft-bristled brush, graduating into meat-flavored paste you could order, see below. David snorted. He wondered how Adrienne would read this: funny or serious?

From the back he heard Blanche yelp. This could be good or bad. Her bark aroused in him a sudden sympathy; she wasn't such a bad dog, really. It was just Adrienne's fixation on her that bothered David. Under any other circumstances she would have been a fine animal, good company and smart to boot. She did exactly what Adrienne said, always. If Adrienne were here now, in fact, he was willing to bet she could command Blanche to be well and the dog would obey.

David's stomach rumbled. He looked at his watch: 1:30. The time surprised him, though which way he could not say. Did it feel earlier? Later? He was hungry, his diarrhea and bad tooth long forgotten. He peered around the corner of the front desk and called out the vet's name. Nothing. He checked his watch again. Still 1:30. He slipped out the door.

Taco Tico would give him diarrhea, he decided, and that would be justice. He ate his burritos, sauce oozing down his chin. He thought about Adrienne's million pictures of Blanche, every stage of the way. First, Blanche changed the most, grew through puppyhood while Adrienne stayed the same, her high school hair stringy and close to her head. Then Blanche stayed the same for a few years while Adrienne changed, went from chubby to thin, then settled for medium, her hair growing longer, getting stringier, then shrinking against her head, getting permed, then growing into medium also. There was a picture with the two of them in earrings, Adrienne both sides, Blanche only one. For a while they both stayed about the same. Then Blanche got grayer, chunkier, shorter, if that was possible. Her tongue hung out more and her eyes got wider. Her face turned white. Her legs bowed. She looked a little desperate. Adrienne remained tall, medium, smiling, hair and eyes the same: young, basically.

David dropped his tray into the trashcan accidentally and left it there.

Back at the vet's, nothing had changed. He considered tapping the bell on the desk, then thought he'd rather not know, really, if something had changed. Eventually the doctor emerged, pulling a rubber glove from her hand as if she were a real doctor. David felt scorn, then corrected himself. She *was* a real doctor. Even vets wore gloves. He waited for her to speak.

"We'll keep her overnight and see what we can do. She's had a stroke."

David drove home, Blanche's leash beside him on the front seat. If Adrienne had come home while he was gone she would have put two and two together: spilled drink, bathroom a wreck, car gone, dog gone. But she wasn't there, the mess was still intact. He cleaned up, wiping the tub smooth, washing Blanche's honey hairs and sand down the drain, throwing all the towels in the machine after he soaked Bloody Mary out of the carpet with them. The phone rang; David's heart leaped over a few beats.

"Hey, how's the boy?" It was Robinson, calling from the Stivaks' pool house phone.

"I'm all right. But my wife's dog had a stroke." David undressed while they talked, wanting to get back to his bathrobe for some reason.

"I thought that was a human problem."

Human problems, David thought. "Nope. It can be a dog problem, too."

"Well," Robinson said, then didn't follow up.

"I'll see you tomorrow, for sure," David said. "I know I'll be better."

"Okay. Sorry about your dog, man."

"Yeah."

"Bah."

When he heard Adrienne's key in the lock he realized he shouldn't be in his bathrobe. How would she believe he'd taken the dog to the vet if he was wearing his bathrobe? He grabbed his clothes from the hamper and ran into the bathroom just as she called for Blanche.

At four-thirty they both sat in the familiar waiting room, Adrienne's fingers dug into David's wrist. There was no word on Blanche. The clinic was supposed to close at six, but the doctor would stay with Blanche all night if necessary. David had listened without really believing it: the vet would stay all night for the dog. It didn't surprise Adrienne a bit.

"What happened to the stray?" he asked, to distract her.

She was staring at the toothpaste poster, uncomprehending. "Oh, it's really pretty interesting," she said, not interested at all. Her eyes were miserable from crying, her face contorted. She was ugly, David thought briefly.

"Tell me," he insisted.

She took in a lungful of air. "Well, I found the dog again, but he was running down this alley. I followed him and he ran into this yard. I didn't want to go in, you know, in case somebody was home, but . . ."

"Go on."

"So I squatted down and I called him, tempting him with dog food." She stopped to calm her tears. Blanche's dog food. David patted her with his free hand. "But he wouldn't come, so I threw some to him. He ate it and I threw more, each time getting it closer and closer to me. Then this cat showed up, this huge cat, bigger than the dog, and she started eating the dog food. You should have seen this yard. I couldn't believe it. What a mess, junk everywhere, toys, wood, a red wagon full of limes. That was the weirdest thing—that wagon full of limes." She snuffled. From one of the cubicles an old woman and man emerged, the woman carrying a black tom, his fur mangled.

"Oh Spike, Spike, Spike," she cooed while the man looked over her shoulder, patting the cat's ridged ear.

The man smiled at them. "If you can't have kids, you have pets," he explained. They paid the receptionist, who would not look David in the eyes.

"So there's the cat and the dog in the yard," David prompted, "with the wagon."

Adrienne watched the couple. "They're so old," she said when they left. "And they love that cat." She sighed, her tears starting up again.

"Come on, Ade, what about the stray?"

"Well . . ." She took a deep breath, enough to finish off the story. "The surprising thing is that the dog and cat got along. So I thought, 'He lives here. He found his way home and I was just following when it happened.' By then I'd come farther into the yard. I knocked on the door and nobody answered, which made sense, because nobody had answered when I called on the phone either, so I figured here he was, home.

There was even a leash tied around the tree, and an empty dog food bowl." She stopped.

"Hmm," David said. An empty dog food bowl, he thought.

"So. So I tied him to his leash, left him the rest of Blanche's food, and walked on to work. The end, I'm thinking. I'm thinking, while I'm walking, what a good deed I've done, how I hoped if anybody ever found Blanche out loose that they'd bring her some food and leave her back in her yard with her cat. If she had a cat."

David laughed, involuntarily. He reached around Adrienne. It occurred to him that if Blanche died he would have a chance, a real chance, at becoming the thing that Adrienne loved most. The thought raced through his blood.

"And I was also thinking how you would like it if I helped this dog, you know? I was thinking about that poem, 'A thing of beauty is a joy' and so on, I don't know why. It doesn't make much . . . " She lifted her toes off the floor, breathed wetly. "Sense. I was thinking helping was a thing of beauty, but it was conscious, which kind of ruins it maybe . . . *Any-way*," Adrienne went on, stronger. "Here's part one of the weird stuff. I call this number from work. Three two six . . . and so on, and this German guy answers. Very old, deaf practically. I say, 'You lost a dog,' and he says, 'Yes?' and I go, 'Well, I tied it up outside your house.' He says nothing. Then he says, 'The voman vill be happy.' I go, 'What?' He goes, 'The voman next door vill be happy.' Turns out they live in a duplex, she doesn't have a phone. Well, I ask him what's his address, and it's the wrong one. It's like half a mile from where I tied the dog up."

"Really?" The plot thickened.

"Really. So I tell why I tied his neighbor's dog up at the wrong house, explaining about the cat and the tree, but who knows what he's understanding, and then I give him the address of the house where the dog is tied up. He can go over there himself and get it, I figure. 2015 East 8th, I tell him. Then I say I'll call back later. Okay, so that's the end of it. I forget the whole thing and work. I was late so I have a lot to catch up on . . ."

"I called you."

"Yeah?"

"She didn't tell you?"

"She wasn't there when I got there. Early lunch. You called about Blanche?" she said.

"Uh huh."

"Oh."

"Go on. What happened next?"

"Anyway, so I forgot all about it until after work. Since it was on the way, I decided I'd stop by and see what was up with the dog. Well, I gave that German man the wrong address—it was on 7th Street, not 8th. 2015 East 7th. God, I thought, what is he going to think? He probably went to the wrong backyard and everything. So I went up to this house, the right house, and the front door was open. Somebody was home. And I wondered what they thought about that dog tied to their tree, you know? I worried that maybe they'd called the pound or something. I looked through the screen and there was this girl, maybe twelve, sitting in a swivel chair staring at the wall. I swear to God, there was nothing around her, nothing she could have been doing. Just staring at the wall." Adrienne sniffed.

"Staring at the wall . . ." David coached.

"I knocked. She kind of came to, really spacy. I told her the whole thing, you know. 'You don't know me, but . . .' She said, 'Just a minute. Let me go see if there's a dog there.' She left me on the porch and went out back. Pretty soon she returns. She says, I swear to God, 'I think that's our Paco.' I say,

'That's *your* dog?' She says, get this, 'I think so. I think that's Paco. Come on in and I'll look again.' So I come into this house, you wouldn't believe it. Junky, but like it's still being constructed, pieces of the walls are missing, a globe on the table, a broken telephone, and dog bowls, which kind of reassures me. I go into the kitchen and out the back door. She's squatted on the ground, holding up the dog's paw—he's still there, tied to the tree, the cat's still walking around—and the girl's checking him out. 'Yeah, I'm pretty sure this is Paco.' What a case, I'm thinking, doesn't know her own dog. Well, I leave my phone number and name. What else can I do? The dog looks happy enough. She says her mom will call me. I'm starting to figure that maybe it *is* the same dog, but with two different owners or something. Maybe they haven't had it long enough to remember what it looks like . . . "

The front bell rang, a boy and his cat came in. The receptionist hustled them into the cubicle the old man and woman had come from. The cat cubicle, David thought. It was nearly closing time.

"What then?" David prompted, gently.

"As I'm walking out the door, she says, 'This has been a strange day. All day long strange things have been happening.' "

"Whoa," David said. Adrienne had cheered a little in the telling, but then the vet came out of the other cubicle, the dog cubicle. She motioned with her finger for Adrienne, who recognized the woman's expression, just as David had. Blanche had died.

They drove home the long way, avoiding the rush hour traffic of main thoroughfares. Adrienne cried and cried; David's eyes teared in response. The vet wouldn't let Adrienne take Blanche home. There was some law about city burials.

". . . and I never let her have puppies, I got her spayed so early on . . ." She cried harder, confessing other non-sins.

"Let's drive by that stray's house," David suggested. "What'd you say, 8th Street?"

"7th." She wiped her nose on her arm. "Oh, David, I've had her so long."

"I know," he said, hoping in some vague way that he did.

They pulled into the alley. Adrienne pointed out the notice on the phone pole: missing dog, small, black with tan markings, red collar. Reward. 326-0775.

"This house," she said, then, "No, one more." A woman with a red bathing cap was emptying her trash across the alley, watching them suspiciously. "This is it," Adrienne said. She had to lean over David to look.

In the backyard, sure enough, was the dog, sitting under a tree, tail curled around him, looking content. Even if he did have another home, he seemed perfectly happy at this one. There were no lights on inside, though a few other lights had gone on next door. Beside the house, with her back to them, seated a few feet from the red wagon full of limes, was a woman. She was playing a blue accordion.

They lay in bed, dinner foregone. Adrienne was beyond crying. She said nothing, clung to David and shivered, then ceased, the way Blanche had earlier. He hadn't told her about the bath (how could that be the cause, he worried, endlessly, how could that possibly be the cause?), hadn't told her he wasn't really sick. He ran his tongue over a tooth that really had begun hurting; inside, he felt loose enough to have the real runs.

"I won't be able to sleep," Adrienne had said, but eventually she did, still clinging to David.

In his dreams, when he finally slept, he saw Blanche, outside for her nightly stool. She circled, as was her habit, for a moment in the corner of the yard, her designated area. She cast a sad but resigned eye at David, who always watched when he took her out, curious. Her legs fanned, her honey-colored fur pale in the dark yard, she lifted her head. The expression on her face had always struck him as oddly peaceful—odd, because it was obvious that she was in pain.

David thought now, dreaming and yet close to waking, that he had willed her death, that he had killed her in order to save himself. He saw Adrienne as a vessel, capable of holding only a limited amount of love. Blanche had syphoned off her share and now it was his turn. He held his wife in his arms, sure that she radiated sufficient heat for the two of them.

Cold Places

Hersh drew circles with her toe at the end of the tub. She had been instructed by her mother to stay upstairs, so she brought the phone into the bathroom, dialed her brother's number in Lawrence, and talked as she soaked. They talked about the East High play; Hersh had a supporting part. She played the mother, as usual—she always tried for the younger roles, but always ended up in the oldest. Dress rehearsal had finished late and had been an especially good one. Her hair was still knotted on her head, and the heavy pancake makeup sweated into her bath water, turning it dirty pink. She told Lee that she was in the tub and he said not to drop the phone in the water. Then he asked about their parents, whose marriage was off and on.

Hersh told him *that* hadn't changed. "Something's happening, though," she said, "because I have to stay up here." When she'd come home, her mother had stepped from the kitchen, closing the door quickly behind her, as if keeping something from escaping. She told Hersh to go upstairs, that she could eat dinner later, although it was already late. "No whining," she had warned.

"What did you just say?" Hersh said.

"I wish things would clear up," Lee repeated. "One way or another."

"*Which* way?"

"I don't know." He had started to fade out.

"Talk into the receiver, Lee."

"I said, I don't know."

Downstairs, a door slammed and plaster trickled inside the bathroom walls. "Something's weird," Hersh said. She quit moving her foot so she could hear better. Lee was silent. Hersh imagined she heard little blizzards on the line between them. Then there was a click; someone had picked up the phone downstairs.

"Where is he?" a woman's voice said, the unmistakable voice of a drunk. "Where is he?"

"Who's that?" Lee said, loud and clear. "What's she doing on our line?"

"Where *is* he?" the woman said. Nobody answered. "I hear you breathing," she said. Then she hung up. Hersh heard another door slam, more plaster crumbling.

"What's she doing in our house?" Lee asked.

"I'll call you back." Hersh leaned over the tub's rim and set the phone in its cradle, her breasts flattened against the cool, wet porcelain. She waited a second before she stood.

Wrapped in a towel, she went halfway downstairs, leaving foot-sized puddles on the floors and steps. Her mother met her on the landing, hands held in front of her as if to push her daughter back upstairs. Instead, she dropped them and leaned against the wall. She started crying, slipping one ineffectual hand in her jeans pocket, one in her short, dark hair.

"What, Mom?"

"Diane," her mother answered.

"Oh." Hersh wondered if that name would ever sound like a normal one again. Diane was her father's mistress. Their affair kept being over, and then not being over. Her father would live at home and then at Diane's and then, sometimes, alone at Motel 6.

"Why'd she come *here?*" Hersh hugged her towel closer, scowled uncomfortably under her makeup.

"Who knows?" her mother said. "She just showed up at the door, saying, 'Marlene, we should talk.'"

Hersh didn't meet her mother's eyes. "So where's Dad?" she asked.

"I think he's at the motel. We were both angry with him. It was an odd scene, Hersh." Her mother let loose of her hair, covered her forehead with her palm. "The three of us," she added.

"I heard you," Hersh said. True, her bathroom was over the kitchen, but all she'd heard were the tones, pitched high and low. It hadn't even occurred to her that Diane's voice was one of them.

Her mother raised her hand like a visor to look more closely at Hersh. "I'm sorry for that," she said.

Hersh shrugged, then smiled to reassure her that it was no problem.

In a new voice, her mother said, "How was rehearsal?"

When she'd left school, Hersh felt she could have run all the way home in the snow, it had gone so well. Her drama teacher had sat in the back of the auditorium, speaking into a tape recorder. Onstage, they knew they were making mistakes when they could hear the click of the machine. Afterwards, he'd said, "I'm not going to tell Hersh to bring her intensity level down—you all have to build up to it." He recommended that the cast take her example. "Become, become," he kept shouting. "Look how Hersh has *become.*"

"It was okay," Hersh said. She began to shiver, felt goose bumps spreading from her chest down her arms. Her jaw, from talking, from clenching, was fatigued. She had, she suddenly remembered, a French paper to write before bed. "So where's Diane?" she asked.

"She left after your father did." Her mother paused, then, again in the other voice, said, "You look nice with your hair up. Your face is such a nice shape. Heart." She smiled and crossed her arms. "But that gray is terrible."

"It takes three days to wash out, too. And then there's more to put in before the show." Hersh imagined she and her mother could still share a normal night, talking in these voices, sitting at the kitchen table drinking tea and writing her paper.

"Well," her mother said, and her voice shifted, the conversation with Diane returning to her eyes. "I have to look for your father. You go get back in the tub. You're freezing."

Hersh nodded. She went upstairs and into the bathroom. The water felt better than it had before, hotter. Her aeronautics teacher always said you had to know the bad before the good looked good. You have to know the cold of this house in winter, Hersh thought, before you feel the hot of a bathtub. She lay back and rested her head against the rim. She soaked a washcloth and spread it over her chest, something she used to do when she was younger, taking bubble baths. She'd pretend a long line of men were waiting to kiss her. She'd indicate she was ready for the next one in line by raising a bubble-covered finger.

Outside, her mother's Falcon whirred and hacked to life. Inside, Hersh felt at the center of some disseminating structure. Here she was in the bathroom, in their house, in Wichita, in Kansas, the middle of the country. Away from her were her older sister, over to the left, in Denver, and Lee, to the right, in Lawrence. She heard her mother drive off.

What would her sister do if she were here? Hersh pictured Paige coming home and her mother herding her upstairs. Paige, the oldest, five years older than Hersh, would have sneaked back down and listened in on the conversation as if it were her right. She might not have been able to resist entering it. Even if she had resisted, on the landing Paige would have asked precisely what was going on. Her mother would have wanted Paige's advice, and there would have been a lengthy conversation about her father's lack of self-awareness. Hersh wondered why it was she could predict what Paige would do and yet still not do that thing herself. She reached for the phone to call Lee back.

"Well?" he said. She told him what she knew, which wasn't much. They sighed.

"Do you talk to people about this?" she asked.

"The affair . . . ? No."

"Why not?"

"I don't know," Lee said. Hersh pictured him looking at his shoes, elbows on his knees, fist under a red cheek.

"I almost told Lucy," Hersh said. "But I can't tell her who." Diane worked at East High, teaching government. "Lucy has her class next semester."

"Paige had her," Lee said. They were quiet again. Since they'd found out about their parents' problems, last summer, the enormity of it had overshadowed the other parts of their lives. Hersh felt selfish discussing school. Or almost anything else.

"It's like cancer," she said. "We can't talk about our friends or music or whatever because of it. Just like someone dying."

Lee laughed. At another time he might have corrected her: cancer and death aren't the same thing, he would have said. You act as if they're cause and effect.

Suddenly Hersh heard noise on the steps. "Lee," she hissed. She listened again. It was her father, she could tell by the way the steps creaked, his pace.

"Are you sure it's him?" Lee said.

She was sure. Her father walked down the hall and passed

the bathroom door. She could almost feel his shadow go by. He went into her bedroom. "He's in my room," she said.

"*Your* room?"

Neither of them could figure it out. Hersh wanted to get out of the tub and lock the bathroom door; it seemed to her the only safe place in the house, the only place no one except her had been in tonight.

"I think he's hiding in there," Hersh said. From what? she wondered. Lines from rehearsal ran through her mind. *You must behave yourself. Anna, don't play like that. It's not dignified.*

"God," Lee said.

"I'm going to go," Hersh said. "I'll find out what's what and call you back."

"Okay," Lee said. He was getting his phone voice, speaking with the receiver at his throat. Far away, Hersh heard, "Goodbye."

She got dressed. She pulled the plug and let the pink tub water gurgle away. Her clothing felt heavy and oily against her clean skin. If her father weren't in her room, she could roll into her heaps of blankets, curl and burrow, discover tomorrow how the night had worked itself out.

Downstairs, all the lights were on, as if a party were about to begin. Hersh walked around—living room, dining room, kitchen—waiting to be startled. In the kitchen, she listened to the ceiling. Her father was still up there. She wondered if he was sitting on the floor. She thought he was probably sitting right by the radiator.

A green thermos Hersh didn't recognize lay on its side on the table. She remembered a poem she'd read about a jar on a hill. She hadn't understood why it was a poem, what made it a poem in a book. She shook the thermos. Empty. *Anna,* her character said, *don't play like that.* She held the thermos the way her character would, like a treasure. *Remember*, her drama teacher said. *You're starving, living on rations.* Suddenly the front doorbell started ringing, again and again. The dog, Dolores, howled from the living room. Hersh considered letting the bell ring until whoever was there gave up, but neither Dolores nor the person would stop. She went to the door.

"*Hush.*" Dolores stopped, but continued to swish her tail angrily. Hersh pulled the bolts. There stood Diane, on their front porch with no coat on. It must have been near zero outside.

"Somebody stole my car," she said. She was younger than Hersh's mother, and much smaller. She wore her long red hair straight down her back, where it hung like fringe. The boys at East High whistled at her. She and Hersh ignored each other in the halls, and Hersh had had to petition out of her class, though she couldn't tell the administrators why. Everybody knows, Hersh thought, but nobody says.

Diane didn't seem to recognize her, just kept talking as if she'd begun before the door opened. "Somebody stole my car, it's gone, goddamnit, I looked everywhere." The snow on her boots melted into puddles on the mat. Her clothing was all snowy and wet, and she slumped like something dead; she looked to Hersh as if she were melting. "Hey." Diane narrowed her eyes, thinking of something. "Your dad took my car!"

If she told Diane her father was in her room, Diane would march up there and get him out. They would go look for her car together. Hersh would lock all the doors after they had left and call Lee with an update. Or, if Diane went up there and her father refused to come out, they would shout at each other. Or she would go in Hersh's room and they would make love, right on Hersh's bed. Really, there seemed to be no end to what might happen if Diane went upstairs. Hersh wondered if Diane had ever been upstairs in their house before, in her parents' room, looking through her mother's things, lying in their bed.

"He wouldn't steal your car," she said, stepping out onto the porch. She decided Diane wasn't coming back in their house, even if she was so cold she melted and then refroze. "He wouldn't do that," Hersh repeated, but she thought, *He could do anything.*

Diane said, "That's my thermos." Hersh looked down and was surprised to see the thermos in her hand. She gave it to Diane, who immediately dropped it on the brick porch. "Oh hell," she said, and began sobbing, her whole body heaving.

In the play, Hersh's character stood for no nonsense. This sort of crying called for a slap across the face and a sharp reprimand. *Stop this at once!* she would say, and shake the crier's shoulders. To Diane, Hersh said, "We can drive around and look for your car." Diane just nodded.

They'd driven two blocks before Hersh realized she didn't know what Diane's car looked like. "It's a compact, yellow, with a dented fender," Diane told her. "Which was not my fault. My son . . ." Hersh looked over, but Diane was staring out the window. "Hard to believe this, hard to believe," she said.

They drove up First, down Quentin, up Douglas, down Bluff. No car. Diane slumped in her seat, boneless and silent, as if asleep. Several times the car skidded and weaved on the ice, but Hersh knew that nothing more could happen. The odds said nothing more could happen in one night. Diane leaned forward slowly until her forehead touched the dashboard. She seemed to be speaking to herself. "He doesn't love *her*; he loves that *house.*"

Hersh realized that this could be true. The house was enormous, eighty years old, and full of furniture and repairs her father had made. Even Lee, away at school, talked about how much he missed the house. Everybody in the family had separate rooms and places for themselves. A couple of times in the last year her father had lived in the house but without seeing her mother: he'd stayed in the guest room, altered his schedule to eat alone in the kitchen. Hersh had only recently understood that all this space was a luxury. Her sister Paige once said she thought their parents' problems would have been resolved long ago if they lived in an apartment. She thought space allowed them corners in which they could avoid the issue.

"Where's your house?" Hersh asked Diane. They had covered six blocks without finding her car. The smell of stale liquor was giving Hersh a headache, and she cracked the window. Then she remembered that Diane didn't have a coat, so she rolled the window back up. She tried to think what it was like before she'd found out about her father and Diane. What had she thought about a year ago? About virginity? About her terrible habit of staring at men's crotches? The car slid around another corner. Filthy snow was piled at the curbs.

Diane rested her ear on the dashboard to face Hersh. She told her where her house was; it was closer than Hersh had thought. "Somebody stole my car. Just another goddamned thing to worry about," Diane said. "Another goddamned thing." She reached across and poked the cigarette lighter. When it popped out, she pushed it back in. Over and over. "You know what he told me? He told me you needed him around. That you were buddies, you did things together. But I can tell you don't do things with him. That would be pretty unlikely, a seventeen-year-old and her dad doing things together." She shook her head, looked out at the snow. "Right?"

Hersh thought about it. "Sometimes we make bread," she said. They would shut off the kitchen and turn on Sunday opera. Hersh assembled the ingredients; her father mixed and told her the plot to the opera. "That's about it," she added.

Diane nodded, tired, disgusted. She pointed. "There's my house."

All the lights were on there, too. Next door to Diane's, the curtains were open and Hersh could see some people sitting in reclining chairs facing the street, watching television. She knew their house would be warm, the thermostat on 80, and she alternated between wanting to be in the room watching TV with them and wanting to yell at them, tell them what was going on outside, next door.

Diane couldn't find the door handle, and to avoid touching her Hersh climbed out of the car and went around to open the door. She worked on moving slowly, practicing for the play. She held the door for Diane, who pulled herself out and then tripped up the sidewalk to her porch, where she turned around. "No keys," she yelled. "And where's my thermos?"

Hersh found the thermos on the floor. When she picked it up, the broken glass lining rattled. "Useless," she said, but took it to Diane, who, in search of her key, had dumped the contents of her purse on the porch. She and Hersh had begun picking through the mess when the door opened. Diane's son Carl stood there barefooted, his corduroy pants low on his hips, his face foggy with sleep. He didn't say anything, just turned around and dropped solidly onto the couch.

Diane gathered everything clumsily into her hands and said, "Come in."

The TV was on, but it was a recorded show and the machine had stopped. A close-up of Dan Rather's face wobbled on the screen without sound.

"Will you wait a second?" Diane said to Hersh, and then shook Carl awake. "Get up, hon," she said. "We have to find the car." He looked at both of them, and then at the TV. He had graduated from East High the year before, just barely. Hersh knew him by reputation only, wild, dumb. He picked up the TV control box and with a little sweep clicked Dan Rather off the screen. His height and thinness and blond hair reminded Hersh of pale tapered candles.

Diane went into another room and started dialing a phone. Hersh stood awkwardly, wondering where her father sat when he came over, which one was his chair. "She's sort of drunk," she said, by way of explanation. Carl shrugged. Suddenly she remembered the gray in her hair. Horrified, she reached up and felt her stiff bun, like a hat, on her head. But Carl wasn't paying any attention.

"That's my car she's talking about, you know," he said. He combed his hair with his fingers. There were red marks on his cheeks from the couch.

"It's not stolen, I don't think," Hersh said.

"Oh, yeah? Where do you think it is, then?" Carl asked, nastily.

"I don't know," she said. Instead of being angry, she felt she could begin crying any minute. She steeled her lips. *Purse them!* her drama teacher said. *Become a hard-ass. This old gal's a hard-ass!*

Diane came back in with the phone. "I'll call till he answers," she said. Hersh wondered where she'd dialed, where she thought he was. They all stood there for a moment, and then Hersh set the broken thermos on the coffee table and said goodbye.

She was halfway down the front walk, on her way home to bed, when Carl yelled at her. "I want to look for it," he said. "Drive me over there, okay?" He ran down the walk carrying his shoes and jacket. The shoes were enormous. In the car he asked where the knob was to adjust the seat. He took up quite a lot of room, and when he set his foot on the dashboard to put on the shoe, his knee went over his shoulder.

"My dad is at our house," Hersh said. "He didn't take your car."

"Who said he did?" Carl said. The night was bright with snow. They could see everything. They slid when Hersh changed lanes, and then again when she rounded Circle Drive. "She's always doing some dumbshit thing," he added.

Hersh liked him a little better for this. She was tempted to ask, "What other dumbshit things?" That would be what her sister wanted to know. Instead, she said, "You know why we can't have an accident tonight? Because so much has happened that it couldn't get worse."

"Come on," he said. "You could have an accident real easy tonight." He laughed. "It's slick as shit. You could wreck in a second." He snapped his fingers. Hersh blushed. If she'd told Lee, he would have understood. What did her father find to say to this boy? Did he laugh at her father's stories? Did he embarrass her father? "I totaled our last car right here," Carl said. He turned to watch the intersection go by. "That was a sad day."

Fine, frozen snow blew in the streets, like dry ice. There were fewer cars out, almost none parked anywhere. It was getting late; house lights were going off. Carl kept wiping his window to clear the fog. Tomorrow, Hersh knew, she would see his fingerprints on the passenger window. Would she tell Lucy? Point to the fingerprints and say, "You won't believe this?" But then she'd have to say who it had been, and that would lead to Diane. She only had Lee to tell. Or she could call Paige in Denver. She pretended Paige was watching her drive. She tried to relax. "See anything?" she said.

"You'll be the first to know."

Hersh ran through questions she couldn't ask him (How long have you known? Where is your father? Do you like my father? Why do you live at home? What do you do all day?). "Did you ever go to any plays?" she decided on.

"Plays?" he said. "Oh, at school." He drew his lips back like a horse. "Nope. Your dad talks about them all the time, though. He says you're good."

"Really?" She regretted it as soon as she said it; she sounded like she was gloating. But what was her father doing, talking about her?

"Really," he said. "Ever eaten there?" He pointed at an all-night diner, Hot Sam's. "Great barbecue." Through the steamy windows of the diner they could see three men hunched at the counter. "You make a big mess when you eat, grease and sauce everywhere. I love barbecue."

"So does Lee," Hersh said.

"And who's he?" Carl asked. "The cousin or the brother?"

"Brother," she said.

"So the brother is the university one and the cousin works construction."

"Right." *And the mother runs a bookstore, the father teaches college.*

"I remember Lee," Carl snorted. "We were in shop together sophomore year. He wasn't so bad, but his *friends*. The worst."

Hersh started to defend Lee's friends, then decided to agree because she'd often felt the same way herself. Then she just didn't say anything. They came to a stop sign, but slid through.

Carl said, "You're a better driver than he says."

"What?"

"Your dad likes to tell about riding with you. You listen to the radio too loud. And you kill the engine in first gear."

"At least I haven't had a wreck."

"Only because we're the only car out tonight."

Hersh said, "Look down that street. Is it there?"

He turned and wiped his window again. "Negative." Then neither of them spoke.

What if they didn't find the car? Hersh imagined driving through her neighborhood all night, checking the back streets, dead ends, and cul-de-sacs, eventually garages. Or they could start in the other neighborhoods, downtown. Where would a drunk mistress park? How far could she walk on ice? It was all a mystery to Hersh.

At the next corner, she considered turning the other direction, moving west, toward the highway. What if she and Carl just drove off to Colorado? They'd arrive in Denver tomorrow and if someone asked them what they were up to, how would they explain their relationship? She looked over at Carl and tried to imagine kissing him. He looked at her and wrinkled his forehead. "What?" he said. She couldn't imagine kissing him.

"Hey!" he yelled. "Stop, stop! There it is." He rolled down the window and stuck his arm out. A lone yellow Toyota sat in the Safeway parking lot, its windows showing the scantest bit of snow drift. Hersh felt both relieved and disappointed—which the most? she wondered—that the night had ended. Then she remembered her father in her bedroom, her mother off somewhere else. Her stomach tensed again; the night hadn't ended.

"Well," she said. *Well well well.* Safeway was at least half a mile from Hersh's house, a mile from Carl's. "She walked a long way," she said, imagining Diane on the ice, without her coat, coming to see Hersh's father.

"You can do a lot of things drunk," he said. She pulled up next to the car, and they sat for a second. In the Safeway windows were pictures of bright green vegetables on sale. *How dare you steal bread from us,* her character cried, *from the children.* "My license is suspended," Carl said. "Too many tickets."

Hersh sighed. "What do you want to do?"

"I'll drive it," he said.

"You could say it was an emergency," Hersh said.

Carl laughed at her. "They've heard everything. They wouldn't believe it. *I* wouldn't believe it if I heard it. I'd say, 'Come on, punk, in the car, you're history.' " He laughed again. In the parking lot lighting, Hersh saw that his cheek still had indentations from the couch. She saw he didn't even shave yet, just like Lee.

Carl opened his door and had one foot out. He looked at Hersh and squinted. He reached toward her face and she instinctively jerked her head back, hitting the window. "Hey," he said, touching her forehead. "What's this?"

Hersh felt herself blush. She put her hand to her forehead. Stage makeup came off, pancake base, eyeliner. "Wrinkles," she said. "I'm an old lady in the play. Mrs. Frank." They looked at each other. *All this time we thought it was rats.* Just a couple of hours ago she was at school, onstage hugging Tom Filarecki, who played Mr. Frank. He became nervous and sweaty when they had to lie on the pallet together. During rehearsal he'd said lines from their last play and she had had to coach him.

If Carl didn't get out, she was going to cry. He wiped his finger on his jeans. Both of them watched the snow blow against his car. "I hope it starts," he said.

"It'll start," she said. She thought about the night. "It'll probably start."

He slammed the door when he got out, and stomped over to the Toyota. Hersh watched him slap the snow off the windows and climb in. The car started and he roared off across the lot, spinning several donuts before he pulled onto the empty street.

Driving home, she invented omens. If the light ahead stayed green until she had gone through, her mother would be home. If the light turned yellow, her mother would be gone. The light stayed green. If she didn't see another car before she got home, her father would not be in her bedroom; if she saw another car, he would still be there. No cars. She pulled into their driveway, sliding up it at an angle. Her mother's green Falcon was not under the carport, which confused her omens.

Their house was now the only one in the neighborhood with lights on. Her bedroom window was unlit, though. She imagined her father sitting by the heater, in the dark, resting his head on his crossed arms. She stepped out of the car and shut the door, listened to the ticking of the engine. She could have stayed out all night; no one was keeping tabs.

The back door was unlocked and the phone was ringing, echoing through the house like a fire alarm. "Diane," Hersh whispered. She picked up the phone, but said nothing, and heard nothing. Then the line clicked and she hung up. She cleared glasses from the table, rinsed them, and walked through the house turning off lights and locking doors. She felt tired, as if she'd cleaned the whole house that night. She went upstairs; there were still puddles of bath water on the steps and her towel was still draped over the phone desk. Still a mess, she thought. The phone cord led into the bathroom.

She opened her bedroom door and listened to the dark. "Dad?" she said. "I hear you *breathing*," she added, but it was a lie. She couldn't hear a thing. She shut the door. *Don't draw attention to yourself,* her drama teacher said, *when it's not your scene.*

Back in the bathroom, she looked in the mirror. Her make-

up was smeared where Carl had touched her, more of his fingerprints. Really, she didn't look like an old woman at all,
even from the back of an auditorium. She pulled the skin tight
on her forehead. The makeup flaked and filled her own—
tiny—wrinkles. She picked up the phone and dialed Lee's
number, beginning to undress, shifting the receiver as she
pulled at sleeves, buttons. Her brother's phone rang and rang.
After turning off the light, she got into the empty tub. She
didn't run water. Lee's phone kept ringing in Lawrence.
Finally Hersh hung up.

The dry porcelain of the tub warmed only briefly where her
skin touched; the rest remained cold. Hersh hugged her knees
up to her chest, a perfect, still oval. *Don't call attention to
yourself,* she remembered. *Don't distract.*

Outside, dry snow flicked against the window, a reminder
of the freezing night. When she shut her eyes, she saw Carl's
car, spinning on the parking lot. She saw Diane on the front
porch, her mother on the landing, both crying. She shivered
without being able to stop. This is how it goes, she thought.
You come in from a cold place and sit in another cold place.

When the phone rang, she grabbed the receiver before it
could finish. She held it to her ear without speaking.

"Hello?" Lee said, far away. "Hello, Hersh?"

"God, Lee, where were you?" She stretched her legs forward, leaned her head back, reclined for a long talk.

Affair Lite

"It's the three girls," Elaine heard Gerald say to his son Zuther. Elaine looked down at her two companions, her dog and daughter, who both stared at their feet. "Shall we let them in out of the snow?"

The little boy was still nodding when the door opened, his hands together in front of him, the end of a clap. He seemed able to do nothing more than beam at his friend and guest, one-year-old Alice Pitt. For her part, Alice simply stood motionless on the landing and eventually had to be pushed in by the back of her snowsuit by Elaine, who pulled the dog in after her.

"Trepidatious, are we?" Gerald said to Alice. He had instantly sunk to his knees to remove her from her suit. Alice eyed him somberly, her nose running from the cold.

"Gay?" she now said, swiveling her head to locate her mother, who'd gone to drop her own coat and the dog's leash in the living room. "Gay?" she repeated, a bit panicked.

"Oh God, careful, Gerald," Elaine called. "She's got an egg in there somewhere. *Egg*, darling. Say *egg*. She found it in the snow on the way over."

"Gay," Alice said to Gerald. From the inner pocket of her red snowsuit she produced a tiny milk-blue egg and held it in her palm for him to admire.

"Aren't you the little nest-robber!" Gerald said, delighted. "It's a wonderful egg, my sweet. It's a robin's egg. Careful,

Zuth." Zuther had reappeared with his latest toy, a twenty-wheeled caterpillar sort of thing that ran on batteries and could go over anything. He set it down to demonstrate, but was preempted by the egg, which his father now set delicately, in a drinking glass, on the middle of the kitchen table.

"It's a robin egg, Dad. I'll let you turn this on," Zuther offered Alice. "I'll let you run over me," he pleaded, following her faltering steps into the other room. He would try to herd her, but she would have none of it, powerful with her disinterest in his new toy.

"Sit down," Gerald said to *his* guest.

For their parts, the dogs stuck to the hall. It was a marvelous hall, long and wood-floored, with several shut doors on either side. The walls were papered in an aging design of pale violets and faded pansies, pieces of which sometimes fluttered off like old skin. The light fixture was also of flowers, rosebuds on peach-colored glass, located at the point where the hall made a gentle curve toward the bedroom, beckoning. All those closed doors and then the open one. The hallway was the only interesting architectural accomplishment in Gerald's apartment, with its doorways, hopeful in their implicit promise of choices, of other lives behind them.

The dogs, Gerald's male mutt and Elaine's female lab, mostly paced. They had been neutered and spayed, respectively, and so suffered only a benignly confused sexual tension: *What* is it we do? First they paced circles around one another and then they paced the floor plan—kitchen, living room (which was also Zuther's bedroom), master bedroom, bathroom, hall. They then confined themselves to the hall, where they enjoyed sniffing the permanently-shut doors and rooting in the worn carpeting between pacing. They were comfortable friends, having known each other longer, really, than the four people had. The dogs had begun having walks

together almost two years earlier, Elaine's husband and
Gerald taking them to the park when Elaine was pregnant.

"What did you and John talk about when you walked the
dogs?" Elaine asked Gerald now. She sat at his cluttered
kitchen table drinking coffee.

"Pregnancy," Gerald said. "Fatherhood. He was quite worried. Something about his own father, some disaster with a
sports activity. All very hazy to me now."

"Hmmm."

Gerald was making himself a cup of coffee and didn't turn
to look at her when he spoke. Elaine studied him the way she
did her husband—with eyes unable to be objective. Would he
be attractive to someone who didn't know him? Surely his
smile-lined face would appeal? The limber way he moved,
joints flexible as a monkey's? And though his hair was gray, it
was still thick and plentiful, unprofessionally cut, swirling
from a point in the back of his head like the whorl of a
fingerprint.

"What's that?" he turned around and asked in a way that
hoped to be taken casually.

Elaine slipped a heretofore unmentioned Marshall Field bag
farther beneath her chair. She wasn't yet ready to talk about
it. In the bag, clean but crumpled, was an olive-green corduroy
maternity dress Gerald had lent her a few days after meeting
her. He'd gotten custody of it in his divorce settlement. Elaine
was relieved to be returning the dress. It had started not a few
of her problems, beginning on the night she met Gerald. She
and John had given him and then-one-year-old Zuther a ride
home from a party, the kind of party where children are set
down on the floor before the circle of adults and passed off as
the evening's entertainment. John hated such evenings. He'd
wanted to have at least one reasonable conversation, but it
hadn't been possible. Because Elaine had then been five
months pregnant and she knew John saw the whole party as a

vision of his life to come, the evening depressed her. Anybody who had children at the party seemed to be having a marvelous time—it was just after Christmas and there was no end to the toys with batteries and noisemakers; she remembered in particular a fire engine that shot water from a hose—while she, conscious of John's irritation, sat miserably next to him on the sofa feeling she might begin crying.

After the party they gave Gerald and Zuther a ride home in a beginning snowstorm. Somehow John wound up in the backseat with the little boy, while Elaine drove and Gerald sat beside her, telling her about his dog and about Zuther's infancy. They were her favorite topics at the time, animals and babies, and John had grown bored with both. Before she realized she'd made all the right turns, she found herself at Gerald's apartment building, which was, as he'd promised, only a few blocks from theirs. While he extracted sleepy Zuther from the backseat, Elaine remembered she'd walked by his building before.

"I know this place," she said. "There's a white cat in the garden apartment, isn't there?"

"Yes," Gerald said, leaning back into the open car door and smiling at her. She was turned, awkward in the shoulder harness, trying to see the window she'd noticed the cat in, and they looked one another in the eyes, sideways like that.

"What size are you?" Gerald had asked suddenly, Zuther dangling in his arms, snow sticking in his hair. "Medium? Maybe medium-small?" He'd squinted as if to estimate. It struck Elaine as both a generous (because, currently, she was more medium-large) and personal question, calling attention to her pregnancy without, somehow, denying flirtation. "I have a dress," he'd said.

Gerald's kitchen had the temporary feel of a beach house. Its three big windows were new and cheap and dirty already with Zuther's fingerprints and breath-fog writing. They looked out over a ravine where the east-west commuter train ran in the evenings. In the corner three small cockatiels slept on their perch. Beneath the cage was a ridiculously high stack of newspapers. It grew disproportionate to need. His kitchen was as cluttered as Elaine's was clean; he saved, and Elaine threw away. They had, she noticed, instilled in their children these same qualities. While Zuther had filled rooms with his things, Alice would learn that she had to give up her toys as she outgrew them. Squeeze toys were, even now, on their way out. John couldn't stand the *stuff* of childhood, the mess and accumulation of it, the endless stooping to get it up off the apartment's floor, and neither, frankly, could Elaine, though it tore her to give away Alice's first rattle.

"You don't have to return that, you know," Gerald said, nodding toward the dress bag. "It's good with your eyes. Besides, I'm getting old. I probably won't know any more pregnant women."

"Well, my regular clothes finally fit again. And I won't be pregnant anytime soon." She looked away from Gerald, suddenly struck by what he'd said and how she'd responded. He most likely wouldn't know, intimately, many more pregnant women, while she would be pregnant again, would have other children. That part of their lives crossed now, but would not forever. "It's probably best if I leave it here. We try to keep things at a minimum over there, you know." She reached under her and handed him the bag.

"Yes, I'd heard about that, that Zen life-style you lead." He shook the dress out and held it before him. "I've known three women pregnant in this dress. There was the original owner, of course, whose husband went out and vasectomized after their baby. Then came Zuther's mom. We all know what happened there. If only this dress could speak, the stories it'd tell. Friend, wife, near-lover."

Sometimes he called her *diet lover*, or *lover lite*. They hadn't slept together—actually, they *had* slept together, the two of them and their children had on occasion taken a short nap together—but there was no sex, just long afternoons taking walks or drinking coffee or, best of all, lying on the bed next to one another listening to Alice and Zuther. They saw each other nearly every day and between them was the comfortable silence of closeness, of satisfactory mystery. The first time Elaine told him she wanted to lie down with him, he'd led her, smiling, into the bedroom and begun to undress. But she meant it literally; it was the way she always spoke. And they'd lain together dressed, talking. It had been perfect, the precise degree of intimacy Elaine had needed. Gerald kissed her when she let him, curious in a scientific way about the differences between his and John's methods. She decided she preferred to kiss John. But she would stroke Gerald's arm, following the pattern of his slim muscles, watching his cadaverously bony chest rise and fall.

"It's not the sort of dress that goes out of style," Gerald said, rubbing one nappy sleeve between long forefinger and thumb. "I think you could even wear it right now, svelte and all."

"You have to understand the pregnant mind-set," Elaine told him. "I was trapped in that dress for a few months. You wouldn't catch me dead in it now that I have a waist again."

He smiled. "And I thought I understood the pregnant mindset. Silly me."

"Silly you."

"I love pregnant women."

"Why is that?"

"Oh, let's not analyze it. Let's let it be one of my quirks, charming and inexplicable." He poured another cup of coffee for himself and then added half-and-half, which they both watched blend, marble into the hot liquid. When he looked up again, Elaine saw desire and disappointment, simultaneously, in his eyes. He wanted her and would not get her. He had been wanting her for a long while, but she had been pregnant, and then she'd been nursing, recovering, newly in love with John and their baby. It was only now, when Alice was being weaned (beginning to talk) and Elaine found her attention finally turning back to school, perhaps, or to a job downtown at the Art Institute, that sex seemed the looming dark issue. What would it be? his eyes demanded. A full-fledged affair? Affair lite?

It would have been dishonest for Elaine to say John was not an interested parent, though it certainly would have been easier if he weren't. She could have come to Gerald in need of a father for Alice, in need of support for herself. But John loved his daughter. They had a shy and tender sort of affection for one another that Elaine envied. When Alice heard his key in the lock in the evenings, she became jittery, giggling and hiding her eyes, barely able to stand up on her own. When he finally swooped her into the air, she landed breathless, tingling, tongue-tied. She, unlike her mother, would dance with John in front of the stereo. Until she was born, he'd made do with the dog, begging Elaine to join him, but now there was Alice, who performed a sort of nodding and bumping up-and-down step to accompany the bass line. It seemed to Elaine that the older Alice got the more the two of them, she and her father, would be together and the less she, Elaine, would be in the picture.

At Alice's first birthday party two days before, it became clear to Elaine that something would have to give. There were nine children attending, varying in ages, all of them there with a single divorced parent except, of course, the birthday girl. Alice had no real interest in the party—in fact, was made anxious by all the attention she was getting—until Zuther arrived; actually, until Zuther and his father arrived. She was as relieved to see Gerald as Elaine was nervous. He'd been to their apartment only once before, and that had been with John, after an exhausting run with the dogs. Elaine hadn't been home, though for days afterwards she had wondered what he'd made of it, if even then he'd known, as she'd known since the snowy ride home from that first party, that they would discuss her home in the future, share intimacies she was already imagining.

So much of the birthday party depended on the children. What if Alice played only with Zuther? What if she suddenly strung her collection of single words into a lethal full sentence? But what could she say? Elaine herself, adult and articulate, couldn't quite phrase what she felt about Gerald, what happened when she was with him. As she watched him pull Zuther from a jacket and hat—a familiar activity, the undressing and dressing of children in winterwear—she felt a weighty sadness that they hadn't, somehow, met years ago.

But of course that was impossible. Years ago would have meant meeting him before her husband, his ex-wife, their children. All those humans had so much to do with the essential Gerald that Elaine knew they couldn't be foregone, even in fantasy.

Fortunately, Alice turned one year old without a serious hitch. It was later, after the birthday guests had departed, looking as weary and used-up as the remains of the cake and favors, after Gerald had bundled Zuther into his suit and given Alice a slightly longish hug goodbye, when Elaine and John sat on their daughter's bed listening to her pretend to read a new book by the apricot light of her shepherdess lamp—it was then that Elaine understood she would decide. She would have one life and not the other. And still later, in their own bed, the bed whose springs they complained about nightly, the bed they'd accidentally conceived Alice in, the bed they'd come to together for such a long time, her side, his side, lamps, books, water glasses, pillows stained with John's sweat and later tossed off in sleep—it was then, lying curled around her feather pillow and without any desire to do so, that Elaine chose.

Alice and Zuther had macaroni and cheese, their standard lunch, while Elaine and Gerald shared the remains of a lamb stew.

"Bahhhhh," Elaine said.

"Sheep," said her daughter instantly.

"That's very good, Al," Gerald congratulated. "Zuther, tell Alice what the birds say."

"Same old, same old," Zuther said, laughing into his fist.

The birds in the corner were Cookies and Cream and Dearly Departed. They lived with Gerald because his ex-wife was not psychologically able to handle them. That had been the reason Gerald had full custody of Zuther at first, too. Now custody was shared, though the birds remained and though Gerald seemed to have doubts about Zuther's mother's psychological self even now. It upset him to give Zuther to his ex-wife on her allotted days; Gerald would have spent all his time with Zuther, were it possible. It pained him to leave him at daycare. He was the one who suffered the separation crisis, while Zuther went cheerfully to sit in the circle of other three-year-olds, abandoning his father at the door.

Gerald looked at Elaine now and stopped smiling, tilted his head and narrowed his eyes. What's going on up there? he would ask, if they were alone. What's going on in here? he would say, tapping her forehead.

"You have a cold streak," Gerald said when Elaine told him what she'd decided. He then elaborated, as was his habit when something threw him for a loop. "You have a small steel box in your body—who knows where—that doesn't let you give in."

"Give in to what?" she asked, though he sounded so absolutely right to her she had chilled instantly in recognition.

"Give in to your organs, all those mushy fellows, lungs and heart. They can't compete with a steel box. Imagine Alice or Zute trying to fend off a Jeep—little innocent children in the face of mortal metallic danger—and I think you'll have the picture."

They lay on his bed with their hands folded over their rib cages, staring at the ceiling. There was no kissing, no caressing. Elaine heard doors slamming downstairs or across the way. From the living room, where Zuther spent his nights on the couch, stored his clothing in a sideboard, came the piece of another conversation: "The train doesn't go *back*wards, it goes *front*wards, you have to push it this way."

"Someday I'd like to leave out your front door," Alice's mother said to Zuther's father.

"Then you'll have to come without that dog," Zuther's father said, smiling weakly. The lines around his eyes and mouth lifted and fell like those of a marionette, lacking true animation. He hugged Alice tight, a hug to last him, and kissed her nearly closed fontanel very softly.

Walking home, Elaine imagined a box the size of a footlocker, upended inside her, sharp corners poking through at her hips and throat. For a moment, she could not breathe around the cold metal. But then she thought of Alice moving in her, so long ago it seemed, jabbing to test the limits of her world—a soft and vital thing. Elaine looked at her daughter's limbs now, the feet setting themselves one before the other, the arms swinging, and saw they moved with astounding complexity, full of warm fleshy grace.

She could change her mind. But she wouldn't. And then there was that box again. Only this time it wasn't large enough to jut through the confines of her body, not even large enough to be felt on an average day, perhaps only the size of an earring. It was a steel box whose edges were rounding, worn by long-term friction, its gunmetal gray softening to a pewter blue, to a sky blue. It floated tetherless in her system, only at intervals bumping up against a vulnerable organ.

In the course of the walk, little Alice had begun crying. She was stoic in that she continued walking alongside her mother, not breaking down entirely in a heap on the sidewalk, but it was not until they had passed the hospital where Elaine had not given birth, passed the park where, today, the dog was not going to get to run, passed the house where Elaine wasn't going to point out the ceramic squirrels on the roof, and reached the back door of their own apartment building that Elaine understood what her daughter was saying. "We'll find another egg, darling. There will be eggs all summer, don't cry." But she'd begun crying herself by then and so was not much comfort to the little girl.

Mud Season

That first night in the town where her daughter had died, Lois dreamt she was standing in the English countryside. Though she'd never been to England, everything looked just as it should. Green hills dipped back on themselves as far as she could see, stilled waves in a grassy ocean. In this dream, Lois could fly, and she sailed above the ground, taking in the hills and the fine yellow light of sunset, which was so bright she couldn't look at it directly; rather, she had to watch covertly, staring ahead of her while noting it in the periphery.

Suddenly she began rocketing skyward, fast enough to see the world changing before her, slow enough to appreciate the expanding color of the blue sky. Soon she saw a new world, England turning from a borderless countryside into an island all its own. Marvelous. Still, there was that intense light to the west. Perhaps it was not the sun, after all, she thought. Perhaps that was the atomic explosion that would end the world. But, no—its light was yellow and white, painful to the eye but restorative to the skin. Lois knew that if she didn't waken she would continue upward, shooting into some other, dark galaxy. She hesitated, atmosphere thinning around her, before she fought her way from sleep.

She and her husband Alan were staying at a bed and breakfast place in Durango, Colorado. Five months earlier their youngest daughter Gwen had been killed on a mountain pass outside town, not more than a ten-minute drive from where they were. Lois and Alan had come to see the site at last.

Lois looked out their window into the muddy landscape. A boy on a bicycle came slowly meandering down the street, twisting the handlebars from one side to the other, seemingly in order to maintain the slowest speed possible, stalling. He wore bright primary colors, red shirt, yellow cycling pants, blue plastic boots. He wobbled lazily through a puddle while Lois watched, and thereafter left an endless dreamy curve of *S*'s after him.

"What's his name?" Alan shouted to Lois from the shower. "I've forgotten this S.O.B.'s name."

"Pittman," Lois said, dropping the curtain. She spoke only loud enough for her husband to hear her voice and not the word.

"What's it?"

Lois walked into the steam of the bathroom putting an earring in. She pulled the shower curtain completely open and enunciated quite clearly. "Pitt-man." She gave her husband's body a thoughtful appraisal. Do I love you? she wondered. He was small as a pre-teenage boy, skin still almost tight over muscle, but not attractive. The sense of promising vitality beneath the surface was gone. Lois's own body had relaxed into its years. She hadn't really felt comfortable with herself until she'd had children; since then, somehow, her joints and flesh had suited her better. Men's bodies, she thought now, looking at Alan's flaccid penis, never got the chance to ripen—just to age. It was her theory that this was the reason he'd had affairs in the last few years.

Later, over breakfast, Lois confessed that she wasn't sure she wanted to see the site. Her heart had begun beating audibly in her ears, louder as the hour drew near. "Maybe you could go without me."

Alan was pretending to read the paper. He wrote a syndicated column and this paper was open to his small picture and byline. *About Which,* Lois read, upside down. They were running his old pieces while he was away. A little flare of impatience went up in her; Lois thought it would have been more honest to simply let the column go for a week.

"Going will make you feel as if it's done with," Alan said. Maybe he didn't realize he was mimicking their counselor. Or maybe he didn't think Lois would know, since their sessions were separate. Could he possibly believe Dr. Frank came up with completely fresh advice for each of them?

"Actually, I think I'll have this vivid mental image," Lois said, slowly, pinning the feeling. "I think I'll be better able to imagine Gwen flying off the mountain . . . "

Alan turned sharply away. He was contemptuous, staring angrily out the window at the falling snow. What was it this time? Her word choice? He felt bad for her, for both of them, but he could barely stand to be around her anymore. It sometimes seemed hopeless, their marriage. It had seemed that way before Gwen's death, but now it was fated to continue for a while longer, on a different path.

"I'll be okay," she said, waiting until he turned back to the paper before she opened her own section.

Lois believed in human interest stories in the newspaper the way she believed in dreams. She was susceptible to both, drawn to their messages, which she took almost entirely at face value. What did a dream of flying over England mean? It meant she wished to fly over England, to see the earth from a distance. As for the newspaper, her husband's column included stories about his youth, things he saw in a passing car or while standing in the grocery line. He liked to make a point, shaping the tidbits he witnessed into an emotional essay. But over the years Lois realized those columns were awfully overwritten. All the daily pieces were. No one seemed capable of controlling tone. Everything was so unmanageable it all rang false. She believed in straight facts. They spoke for themselves.

These stories sought her out. When she sat in the sunroom in the morning, paper spread on the glass table before her, she had only to slowly turn the pages. Soon the boldface proclamations would rivet her. *Three Sailors Wed Lottery Winner.* Little stories from out-of-state, stories that might get far too much attention if they were local but that only received a cursory paragraph or two of lucid facts if they happened elsewhere. *Baby Found Alive Under El Tracks.* The baby was abandoned, then found after surviving on its own for at least twelve hours. Amazing. Heart-stirring, and without any pomp. *Nurse Playing Hero May Have Killed 10.* A nurse injected patients with lethal drugs, then revived them in order to be a hero. What could be clearer? Why comment further?

Her husband made use of these stories, but only to elucidate some point more specific to himself. Lois imagined if he'd read about the nurse injecting patients he would write about a culture that required heroics and heroes to garner attention. The everyday heroism of nursing was not enough; lifesaving was now necessary in order to receive commendation. That would be the first part of his column—Lois could see it as if it were before her on the page. The next part would be about something comparable in himself. She tried to think what. How had he made himself perversely important in his life?

She admired that he seemed completely able to confess his flaws. All of his readers knew his failures and shortcomings, his sins against himself and others. What bothered her was that, in confessing them, good Catholic he'd once been, he somehow felt absolved.

"Alan," she said, "did you read about this male nurse?"

He had finished reading the paper and was now working the puzzles, his bifocals balanced on his nose. He looked at her through the top part of the lenses expectantly, if a little impatiently, which meant he hadn't. After she'd told him about it, he grunted.

"What does that make you think?" she asked.

"It makes me wonder how the hospital explained away those deaths." He licked his pencil tip and went back to work.

Lois nodded to herself.

But in a moment Alan looked up once more. "It also reminds me of that report that said most serial killers, when asked what profession they'd most like to pursue, answered cop. Remember the ambulance driver who was a mass murderer? Killed prostitutes and then picked the bodies up later the same night?"

Lois did. Alan had speculated on the desire to be a policeman, a surgeon, any occupation that involved day-in, day-out exposure to carnage. He wrote about soaking a cat in gasoline when he was younger, setting it on fire. He'd won an award for that column. It was a brave essay, Lois knew, though it had made their children cry to read it.

"I had the strangest dream," she began. "I took off like a rocket. Usually when I dream of flying I go horizontally, like an airplane. But this morning I was heading up, up and away." Alan was working another puzzle. This one was the one where a sentence was given in code. Each letter stood for another. "Why do you like that puzzle, do you think?" she asked him.

"Couldn't tell you," Alan answered, without raising his eyes. He had been whistling the rhythm of the missing words and discovered the solution in the process. Rapidly, he filled in the last blanks and swung the paper in Lois's direction so she could read the nonsense sentence. *Life of crime can often-time pay overtime.*

"And then I saw a boy on a bicycle," Lois said to herself.

"That whatshisname is going to be here soon," Alan said, rising and running his thumbs between belt and trim stomach. "I believe I'll brush my teeth."

Sheriff Pittman met them in the bed-and-breakfast house foyer. He was kind and slow with them, which made Lois a bit awkward. He had children of his own, she understood. They drove out of town, up the winding mountain road, listening to police static and sudden bursts of dispatched, sputtering numbers on the radio. Lois tried to guess what the numbers stood for, which ones meant robberies, which ones meant fatalities. The sheriff clicked his end of the radio after each, answering in his own code. The scenery—snow filling the deep and high crevices of granite peaks and turning them somehow more than three-dimensional—made her feel unbalanced and she noticed she was holding onto the vinyl of Sheriff Pittman's backseat.

Their waiter at breakfast had told them this snow was unusual, as it was mud season: the end of the ski season, and before the summer tourists arrived. "Other places," he said in his nasal voice, "call it spring." He did not know why they were there, and Lois was grateful for his obvious disdain of people so out of touch as to visit Durango during mud season. She basked in it, the normality of his smugness.

Riding along, she was tempted to tell Alan about something else she'd read at breakfast. A woman had written Dr. Lamb to say she was sick of her husband's habit of eating his own hair. Except she phrased it like this: "He finds the coarse hair on his body, pulls it out, chews it up and swallows it." Lois

wondered if anyone she knew had a habit as shocking. The
atavism of it thrilled her. What would Alan make of it?

But Sheriff Pittman was pulling over, very cautiously, next
to a yellow diamond warning sign. The sign showed a black
arrow bent at a forty-five degree angle. Underneath, it read 2 5
m.p.h. Alan, who was sitting in the front seat, had stared out
the passenger window the whole trip, not noticing the sheriff's glances now and then in his direction. Lois had tried smiling into the rearview mirror to let Pittman know they appreciated his taking care with them, but she had never quite
caught his eye. After all, she told herself, he was a man and he
was identifying more with Alan than with her. Now, Alan
remained for a moment in the car as the other two got out.

Lois had prepared herself to draw in breath, to have her
equilibrium abandon her entirely, her heartbeat become so
furious her body pulsed, but nothing happened. It was a beautiful place, and she stepped right into it. She was not fright-
ened as she walked over to the edge and looked down. What
had she expected? Gwen's body was in Missouri, buried in the
same cemetery with her grandparents and great-aunts. There
was gravel and then the drop, which Lois saw was gentler than
she'd pictured. A squirrel hustled by, holding a nut in its
mouth. At the bottom was no black void where the world had
reclaimed Gwen; up here, no white cross.

She could see how it pained Sheriff Pittman to show them
the spot. He cleared his throat. "There were skid marks," he
said, swiping his cowboy boot heel across the crumbly as-
phalt. "Torn brush and the bent aspen saplings."

Gwen had toppled like a toy the thousand feet. It was Pittman's pain that touched Lois; he certainly must have children
of his own. He must have seen every one of them, in his mind,
make the same horrifying miscalculation, slide and fall. For

herself, Lois had been imagining that fall for months now; it seemed she had been anticipating such a fall since the day she brought her first baby home from the hospital. She'd looked at the world from then on as a place full of forty-five degree angles and cliffs. It surprised her that seeing the actual spot— *here*, she told herself, *right here*—somehow lessened its power. Even the gray sky and wet snow failed to make the turn ominous. An Airstreamer in the far lane rounded it like a ponderous metal elephant. And behind it was the boy on the bicycle. She recognized his yellow pants. Now he bent forward, pedaling hard, a smile—or, more probably, a grimace from the hard work—on his face. Lois lifted her hand in a wave and felt her whole self lift just a bit. She wished she knew his name to call out.

Alan turned to look behind him at what she was waving at. He scowled at her. "I've seen enough," he said. He hadn't even come to the edge. Between them, the sheriff stood with his arms dangling, as if he might draw, also watching Lois. She resisted, the way she had in the car, asking Alan why he didn't want to look over. Their states of mind were at such odds these days that she did not trust his understanding her— something that once she would have taken for granted—and she did not want him to turn away from her as he had at breakfast. So she allowed herself another private glance down. Wildflowers would grow. More squirrels would appear. She hadn't wanted to come, it was true, but now she was glad she had. There was nothing—not the skid marks, not the broken aspen, not the crumpled machine—to indicate what had occurred. This place had healed.

Gwen had missed weeks of class in Boulder, her parents discovered later. They received notes of condolence from several of her professors. The man who taught her Social Problems and American Values course had called one afternoon (teacher's hours, Lois had thought, long distance in the afternoon). He introduced himself and then seemed at a loss. Lois heard, in his silence, the things that could have been between him and Gwen. If Lois had learned nothing else in her life, she had learned to trust what was not said.

"When did you last see her?" she asked him, quiet Peter Somebody or Other, desperate that he not hang up.

"Let me think."

Lois could hear him breathing. He remembered, she could tell, and was trying to put it some way that was presentable to Gwen's mother. They'd been lovers, Lois understood. She wanted to tell him it wasn't his fault. He was tangling with all the little parts—his loyalty to Gwen, his loss, his not knowing Lois at all.

"I saw her at the Union," he chose to say. "She was getting a salad and paying a parking ticket." And then he was silent again. "I don't really know why I called," he said after a moment.

"Thank you, anyway," Lois said. "Even if you don't know, I appreciate it." She was crying, but she thought she could sit for a long time saying nothing with this man.

"It's useless," he finally said, "but what I feel like is that if I could take some of your pain, I would."

"You probably have enough already," she said. "Thank you, though."

She did not tell Alan. She could have secrets, could she not? Alan, fortunately, was gone all day; otherwise, he would have answered the call. She imagined him wanting to reach through the telephone receiver, across all those miles of cable, and strangle Peter Whoever. He would have demanded answers. Why was she in Durango? Where had she gotten a motorcycle, for God's sake? Alan had kept up his campaign against motorcycles, writing column after column about their dangers. They were second only to handguns on his list of consumer evils. It was registered in Gwen's name; she'd owned it for over a year without ever having told them. Alan wanted someone to blame, and Peter, sad and silent, would have sufficed.

Lois had come to admire her daughter's life, secret from the family. She imagined Peter as a kind and older man. Gwen's belongings had been carefully packaged and sent to them, two large boxes that arrived UPS one day when Alan was away. Lois had read the return address, Gwen's dorm, and felt for an instant that she'd been offered a reprieve. Packages from her daughter.

The boxes were full of both familiar and unfamiliar items. Lois picked them up one by one. She couldn't tell which hurt her more to see, those things that were the past or those that were the present. The ceramic rabbit Gwen had had since she was little, cotton balls for a tail? Or the mysterious sky-blue case that snapped open to reveal a diaphragm?

It was not long after Gwen's belongings had come back that Lois stopped wanting to leave the house. Maybe she was waiting for another phone call? She had started any number of days with the intention of going somewhere—the Nelson, the plaza—and had made it through all the preparatory stages, but once she opened the front door she was lost. The world wowed her; leafless trees appeared somehow to be sapping her of energy. It took all her willpower to shut the door behind her and walk to the garage—there was no spark left to actually make her drive away.

Instead, she'd allow herself to be drawn back inside, where she'd gather all the linen napkins in the house to launder them. Their size and texture made for perfect ironing and folding. She was in love with the starchy warmth of these napkins fresh from the dryer. Countless times she comforted herself by sorting them, folding them into perfect squares, her hands flattening, smoothing, stacking, making order out of chaos.

Lois told Dr. Frank about it. It was an "am I crazy?" kind of question. Dr. Frank had pointed to the enormous potted begonia in her window. "That's its third pot," she said. "Every time it gets root-bound it throws itself to the floor and breaks its pot. When that happens, I just have to get it another one. Bigger, of course."

"You think I'm outgrowing my house?" Lois asked. "Like a hermit crab?"

Dr. Frank laughed. "Really, kind of the reverse. You're turning back toward that smaller world. It's healthy, I think. The point is, you seem to be helping yourself by doing what feels right. Warm napkins? They sound lovely."

"They are lovely," Lois said.

If Peter had called again, she would have had something to tell him.

Sheriff Pittman invited them to his house for supper. His wife, he informed them, had been very sorry to hear of their tragedy.

"Quaintly small town, isn't it?" Alan said to Lois, after they'd declined (at Alan's insistence) and the sheriff had driven off. Briefly, Lois pictured a column for *About Which*, eating supper with Durango's sheriff and his wife. The tone would be flat, affectless but affecting nonetheless.

"He's a good person," Lois said, though she too was relieved they would be eating alone. She enjoyed the thought of oblivious strangers, like the boy at breakfast, serving her.

They stood at the inn's entrance and looked up and down the street. It would have been a good time to nap, to pass the two hours before dinner with mindlessness, but they could not sleep. Instead, they walked.

It was Alan who had wanted to come here. Lois had never believed it necessary to see where Gwen had died. She hadn't wanted to see the body either. Alan tried, without success, to make her agree to an open casket ceremony, sure, Lois knew, that he was acting in her best interest. He'd had just enough counseling to know there were things, unpleasant, resistible, one had to do to recover. This trip was in the same vein. He considered traveling, by any means, a dangerous business and he avoided it whenever possible, so Lois knew he felt he had to be here, had to do this. They'd driven to avoid flying, taking a southern route to miss the highest passes. He'd been very nervous (that is, short-tempered) the whole way. Though he'd thought this trip essential, she had agreed only because she wanted him, them, to be cured, to be strong enough to overcome such tremendous odds. The counselor had told her that most marriages did not survive the death of a child. Dr. Frank also suggested that Gwen might have committed suicide. She said this as if she were offering consolation instead of complication. Lois had made her promise not to tell Alan either thing, believing that she could successfully circumvent them, but that he could not.

The two of them wandered the older section of town, Lois peeking into shop windows out of habit. Soon she realized she didn't even know what she was looking at, could not remember whether the place they'd just passed sold antiques or car parts. She put her arm through Alan's for balance, smiling but scared. He did not pat her hand as he once would have. His love was confused, she knew. It tore him this way, that way, distracted him. His latest affair had been longer and more serious than the previous ones, ending only a year ago. He and Lois had still been mending the terrible wounds their marriage had suffered when Gwen was killed. It was like stepping from the foreignness of another country into the alienness of another world. Their grief took hold of them like a merciless wild animal.

And Lois understood that he felt responsible somehow, that he'd pulled his love from the structure of their family and let the edifice slide. His ego allowed him that feeling; he considered himself a cornerstone. He had yet to write about it, and perhaps he never would. It cheered her to think there were some things, however rare, he could not purge.

Now, she felt they were riding some wheel together, that on the far rungs of this wheel they could not touch, could not even know one another. They could only suffer. Eventually she hoped they would work their way toward the center, toward love, where they could be together once more. Alan's affair had created the wheel; Gwen's death enlarged it. They had more distance to come, it seemed, though she believed, finally, that there was no way off for either of them.

Alan stopped suddenly and somehow made Lois drop her arm from his. "I don't think it's too much to want to know why," he said, irritably. "Do you?" He looked hard into her eyes. He was looking to see if she was sane.

"Yes," she told him. It was far too much. That was the whole point. "Look there!" she said suddenly. "That's the third time today I've seen that boy on the bicycle. See his yellow pants? He's like some friendly poltergeist . . . " No, that wasn't it. "Or something."

Alan glanced where she indicated, then slowly turned back to her, his eyebrows and forehead drawn downward in a *V*. But Lois barely noticed, she was so happy to see the boy again.

They sat on opposite sides of a plastic booth in a fast-food restaurant eating chili from styrofoam cups. Of course this was better than being at Sheriff Pittman's, where the only thing everyone had in common was a death. Better to be here, she thought, which could have been downtown Kansas City in winter, snow turning into slush as night fell, headlights and muddy cars passing outside the window, where large cheerful pictures of hamburgers, french fries, and chocolate ice cream hung.

"You think Durango carries the *Times?*" Alan asked her. They hadn't spoken for a long time and Lois's thoughts were far away from the newspaper business. Sometimes, when she and Alan were close, they seemed to think along the same lines and when one of them spoke it was precisely what the other had been thinking, two minds in a winding relay race, passing the baton. Not so today.

"Surely," she said, shifting her thoughts to match his. Reading the paper, she knew, was his way of coping with empty time, idle hands.

She wondered what sort of story the Durango paper had run about Gwen. It had never occurred to her before that there would have been a story, but of course there must. The story in the *Star* had been front-page news, since Alan worked for them. They'd run a photo of Gwen from one of the awards dinners her father had been honored at several years earlier. She'd been clapping, big teeth exposed in a beautiful smile, her sister and brother flanking her at the table. The editor had wanted to rerun one of the columns Alan had written about Gwen, and asked Alan to choose one, but in looking them over Alan realized how many were about her foibles as a safe driver. The story ran alone.

But what had been in this paper? Lois wondered. Perhaps a two-paragraph piece, facts only.

"This was a good idea," Alan said suddenly, their thoughts having gone different ways once more.

Lois considered it. "I don't think we'll know for a while," she said, disagreeing.

He scowled, standing with his plastic brown tray full of trash. "I meant dinner," he said. On the way out, he threw everything in his hands away, tray and all.

At the inn, which had once been the home of a Durango doctor during mining times, Lois and Alan sat on their twin beds staring at the fireplace as if there were a fire in it. There was wood in the grate, newspaper beneath it, long matches in a cup on the mantel. Still, neither of them moved toward lighting it. Lois was thinking of Alan's mistress again, imagining their making love. She was tired and these images came to her when she was too exhausted to fight them. Her friends had rallied round her when Alan was discovered, but then had fallen away when he'd come home again—happier, she supposed, to believe him irretrievable. To put Alan and his mistress from her mind, she tried to remember flying from the night before, the light and the freedom and the frightening unknown. It had been exhilarating, but now there was no fuel left in the memory.

Eventually they turned out the lamp, both in their own beds. It was only nine o'clock. The snow had stopped and they could hear a dog barking in an otherwise still night. Lois attempted to put a good image before her—Gwen walking to class, one of the other children hanging Christmas tree ornaments, the table set for a formal dinner, their own dog barking in their own yard, a boy on a bicycle—but superimposed over them all were those other, awful images.

By morning both she and Alan were in her bed, wrapped together among the sheets and blankets as if they'd wrestled all night for leverage.

They left town before sunrise, taking a different route, at Lois's request, than the one they took when they came. This one would lead them over Monarch Pass. It felt good to Lois to be leaving Durango. Somehow, in the clear melted light of morning, she was comforted in having seen the place, in no longer having to hang onto her imagined site. She couldn't really even recall the accident she had played over and over in her mind. It had disappeared, and a new one, one that included the place Sheriff Pittman had shown them, had yet to come to her. She would fight against its arrival, she decided, sitting beside Alan in the granite-blue of this Colorado morning. If she fought the image hard enough, all day long every day, it would not be able to come in. For a second she could see Gwen's throat, twisted unnaturally, exposed, her youngest, most difficult daughter tumbling down a hillside, new aspens crushed beneath her . . . But she stopped herself, made herself remember only color, blue and red and yellow, and then focus on the scenery outside the car. A fence, the gateposts of a ranch, cows—steam coming from their mouths—clustering at a barn entrance.

When they hit the deer, Lois saw only fur and a single eye before the windshield broke. Its glass rained down on them like pebbles. The deer slid off the hood, leaving a broad smear of blood. "Is it a mother deer?" she whispered to her husband. In a flash she thought of fawns and of full udders, the terrible ache of needing warm milk and needing to provide it.

Alan remained in his seat, staring straight ahead of him, his hands bouncing lightly on the steering wheel, then harder, until the dashboard rocked. He turned on her, his face a horror, red, monstrous. Through his clenched teeth he spat, "Didn't you see antlers? Are you so blind and *stupid* not to have seen antlers? *Mother* deer do not have points. That's *father* deer."

And just as suddenly he fell against her. He cried without tears. She did not know what to do at first, his head against her chest, butting into her again and again, the hard gutteral sobbing. It would have been easier to do in the dark. Even the day they'd heard of Gwen's death, he'd been late at work and she had sat on the back steps waiting for him, her arm around the dog, unwilling to enter the house. When he'd come home, they'd sat there together until it grew dark and then they'd been able to comfort one another.

She tried to soothe him now, running her hand through his hair. The worst had to be over. This would be the last bad thing. After all, it was mud season, that ugly but necessary part in between. She imagined the deer, which she could not see, in front of their car. Perhaps it was alive. But she had no resources; she could not make herself leave Alan to go find out. She pictured its fur as she smoothed her palm over his head. The fur would be sprouting in whorls at its haunches and throat. Its underbelly would be white. There was only so much you could do with one pair of hands, she told herself.

"There can't be any more bad luck," she told Alan in a firm whisper, using a tone of voice she'd once used to promise her children their house would not be robbed, their parents would not die. "We've reached our limits." Alan nodded adamantly into her breasts. "This trip is the end of it," she went on. "*Fin. Goodbye.*"

Not a single car passed. What odds, Lois thought, Alan finally quiet on her lap. The only car on this highway and this deer could not avoid getting hit. Alan would see a column in it, but to her it seemed like a mathematical problem, the kind she used to try to help her children with. In a landscape with only two moving objects in it, how long will it take for them to collide?

Forest rangers on their way to work found them ten minutes later. One of them was young and impatient, shaking his head at their out-of-state license plate, angry with them for having hit the deer. Lois found herself nodding in agreement with his assessment. Careless of them, yes, traveling too fast. They should have known to expect wildlife at sunrise, in the spring, indeed. The other ranger was like Sheriff Pittman, a man who saw them through eyes screened with sympathy and recognition. Perhaps he saw that more than this accident had claimed these two people, both of whom still sat in their broken car, unable to go on.

Looking for
Tower Hall

My wife's family is the most cautious set of drivers I've ever
come across, all except for her little sister Gwen, who was
incautiously killed two Decembers ago on a motorcycle outside Durango, Colorado. No one even knew she was in Durango, much less that she was in possession of a motorcycle.
But their family is like that: slow to reveal what is happening
to them, as if embarrassed, though they would all say they are
close. My wife Tina, for example, didn't bother to let them
know she was pregnant until her mother called on some other
unrelated matter and Tina had to leave the telephone to go
throw up.

So we sit—her mother, father, brother, Tina, and I—in
Tina's car from college stalled in downtown Chicago at rush
hour, none of us having much to say. Everything matches the
car, which is a pea-soup green 1967 Falcon: stormy sky, tu-
multuous Lake Michigan, Tina's maternity pants—everything utility colored. It's a utility sort of month, March. We're
all out looking for Tower Hall. Al used to live in a room there
when he was in the navy, but in the years I've known my
father-in-law, in the few times I've seen him, the navy has
never come up. Al is not one of those men who likes to chew
over WWII. In fact, the only story I have ever heard, outside
this new one about living in Tower Hall, came from Tina.

When Al's father was dying, Al was transported back to Texas in the hatch of a bomber. Where the bombs were to rest, there he lay, trying to sleep.

"I remember marching to Navy Pier," he now says, lowering his window vigorously and craning out. At a stoplight he contemplates the street in both directions. "It was wartime and everyone wearing a uniform was special. But none of this was here. Tower Hall was a brick building with an awning."

"That's half of Chicago," Tina says. With her family, she adopts a city surliness, like a taxi driver with a group of foreigners who can't pronounce their destination.

"After marching on Navy Pier, we marched right over to Rush Street and had a few," Al says, slapping the door through his open window.

"I know I've seen a sign for Tower Hall," says Tina, absently, for she's said this a dozen times now. "One night when we weren't looking for it, we drove right by it. Remember, Tom?"

"No, I don't," I say, sighing. It's as if we could find the building if only we make this exchange the correct number of times.

"Yes, you do," she insists. Into the right lane we swing, drawing a fanfare of car horns from outside and a chorus of hisses from inside. Since Tina's become pregnant, she no longer does head checks when she changes lanes—she says she can feel stretch marks developing if she turns—so her brother Neil has been making them for her. But Neil wasn't fast enough for this latest maneuver. Tina clasps the wheel tighter after her brave move.

"Jee-zus," Al says.

The three of them sit shoulder to shoulder in the front seat, Al keeping an eye out for Tower Hall, Neil telling us the names of the architects whose buildings we're passing, Tina cursing, while her mother and I share, in relative relaxation, the back. Her mother, according to Tina, never used to be so dreamy and quiet, but since Gwen's death she isn't herself. I never spent much time with her before, so it's hard for me to imagine the woman Tina describes—chatty, athletic, a smoker, a bridge-playing, club-joining kind of gossip. Now she seems shy and peaceful as a bird, content to be led by the flock and the status quo. Beside me she smiles sedately—the same smile she has bestowed on everything, indiscriminately.

It was Neil who wanted to visit us. As a way of getting here free, he talked his parents into coming along. All three of them are terrified of flying, and for the first night talked about nothing else. Their fears encourage Tina's own—she told about her own famous near-plane crash twice. (Circling Denver for hours, lightning striking the smaller planes in the air pattern, the woman next to her retching and retching.) Only her sister Gwen was not afraid to fly. Not for statistical reasons, she once told me, just because she liked to look down.

Like most outsiders to a family, I don't understand the trivial they seem to find so fascinating. One more word about flying, I keep thinking, just one more word . . . My own family discusses food. What they've eaten, where. I get postcards from them that Tina finds incomprehensible: *Hello all! We ate buffet tonight—the shrimp was magnificent.* But in my own family, we have so little in common, so little to celebrate when we are together, that food is a natural solution. Eating is our occasion. Correlatively, I suppose, fear is Tina's family's.

I met Gwen twice, once at our wedding and once when she ran away from home. If you saw their pictures, you would hardly be able to distinguish between Tina and Gwen. You would guess twins, though Tina's nearly seven years the elder. You would guess the wrong identity roughly half the time. They both tended to lift their heads when a camera was pointed, as if caught in the middle of a tantalizing bite of wet fruit, taunting, eyes narrowed seductively, mouths a little slack and sweet—a come-hither look. But in person they couldn't have been more distinct. It was as if they'd agreed long ago to divide traits down the middle.

Gwen got the gutsy laugh, the sweeping hand gestures, the outrageous taste in clothes. She got a sort of charming bravado, tempered by two bright red spots that appeared on her cheeks if she happened to overstep that bravado and become suddenly shy. My wife was left with a more serious face, one more likely to watch than take part in conversation. She possesses a quiet solitude, even in crowds. At our wedding I remember the two of them after the ceremony, standing in a group. Gwen swung the straps of her spike-heeled shoes in one hand while waving a glass of champagne in the other, telling a story. Tina, a little drunk, stood next to her happily, arms crossed, watching her sister's mouth or her own feet, pleased merely to listen. I knew, just watching, that Gwen was telling her story mostly to Tina, and that Tina was part of that group, even a group at her own wedding, only because Gwen was there to make it possible.

Around her sister, Tina allowed herself to be childish. They once fought for an hour over the telephone about underwear, about whether Gwen had stolen Tina's during Christmas break the year before. On Gwen's running-away visit, they'd both laughed so hard one night they wet the floor. Gwen had a lolling laziness that encouraged like behavior. She'd stay rolled in a blanket on the couch for most of the morning, watching TV and flipping through fashion magazines, eating honey on saltines. Even Tina, who can't bear to waste time, would be infected. I would come home from work to find them both in long T-shirts drinking beer and playing gin rummy on the rug.

Tina, perhaps because she is an oldest child, has a compulsive need to succeed. She started everything early—from teething to reading to losing her virginity. She graduated a year ahead of every class of which she was a member, finishing graduate school with a doctorate in anthropology when she was only twenty-four. We were married that year, and now, at twenty-six, Tina is pregnant. She feels some need to get on with things, to accomplish them and move forward, competing mercilessly—and is, not surprisingly, devastated by defeat.

This compulsiveness was completely lost on Gwen, who finished everything not only late, but sloppily. In fact, the day the motorcycle skidded sideways over eighty feet of blacktop and then end-over-ended down another thousand feet of cliff was the first day of her final exams at CU. She missed Astronomy and Jazz Movement that day. ("What would a Jazz Movement final be like?" Tina asked me, crying, smiling a drugged, jack-o-lantern smile, beating her fists so hard on my back that I bruised.) Gwen missed Social Problems and American Values the next day, English Composition a few days after. Much later, Al and Lois got a letter from the dean's office telling them Gwen had been failing anyway, that, gradewise, even taking her finals wouldn't have saved her.

After another half hour of slow cruising around Michigan Avenue and the lake streets, Al's ready to admit defeat. "Tower Hall no longer exists," he says. He shrugs, his shoulders tight and angry.

"Oh, it does so," Tina says. "We saw it. Remember, Tom?"

"One night when you weren't looking," says Neil. "We heard. Hey, this is Mies van der Roh Street we're on. Did we miss lunch?"

We go to Sol's Deli, under the El tracks. Fat, cigar-smoking

Sol himself greets us. The first table he offers is in a smoking section and Tina, patting her rounding abdomen, turns it down. The place is jammed and there isn't another clean table open.

"This your daughter?" Sol asks Al conspiratorially.

Al, shy the way Tina is with strangers, nods.

"Daddy's girl," Sol says, indulgently. "I gotta daughter in Arizona, costing me twenty thou a year. You gotta give 'em what they want, don't ya?" He guides us with a pudgy firm hand to a large booth still dirty with someone else's lunch debris. Over the table is a portrait of himself. "How many kids you got?" Sol asks Al.

"Three," Al says, still smiling his shy smile, though the rest of us suddenly somber up. Three? Then Al, too, remembers and his mouth falters.

Sol, still all good spirits, says, "Hey, I got three daughters of my own, each of 'em more expensive than the one before. Lemme recommend the Polish sausage today. It'll grow hair on your chest, I guarantee it. Hey—I even guarantee hair on the unborn!" He rolls off toward the kitchen, nodding at a busboy that our table needs water.

Al spreads the *Tribune* over his part of the formica as if marking a boundary, involving himself in it to avoid looking at the rest of us. In Kansas City he writes a syndicated column for the *Star,* and everywhere else he reads the city dailies, cover to cover.

"Did we eat here before?" Lois asks. She hasn't spoken for so long that she has to clear her throat a time or two.

Tina, sitting next to me, pinches my thigh. Her theory is that her mother is losing her mind. "That was a deli in Rogers Park," she says. "Way north." She nods her forehead vaguely northward. Actually, it isn't just Gwen's death that accounts for what Tina calls her mother's loose-endedness. There'd been a messy affair Al was carrying on, which, though ended now, lingered in everyone's mind.

"You think I should have Polish sausage or Vienna beef?" Neil asks, seriously.

"Both," Tina answers. "Two of each."

"The carnivore," Al contributes, without looking up. "Slaughter the beasts, bring on the meat."

Neil pulls on his hair while searching the plastic-covered menu. For a while he seemed to be a different person every time I met him. At the wedding I thought Neil was aloof and that he disapproved of my marrying his sister. Now I can't imagine having felt that way. He's a gangly man, quiet and with sleepy eyes, always seeming only half there. He is the middle child, twenty-three years old, affable, sandwiched between the contrasting personalities of his sisters like something compliant—marmalade, perhaps. Or mortar. Without Gwen to bookend the other side, however, it's possible Neil feels a little untethered in the family, suddenly cast as the youngest. He's a peacemaker without warring factions. But it's hard to tell how he feels about anything. Conversations with him are stubbornly impersonal. He talks science. He talks buildings. His choosing to visit probably has more to do with the Chicago skyline than with us.

"I wonder what 'Sol' could be short for?" Lois muses.

Al frowns at her. "Solomon," he says. "What else?"

Lois smiles, nods. "Solomon. I see. Tina, is it liverwurst that tastes like pâté?" Lois turns to my wife, holding her half-glasses at her nose with her pinky raised. "Or is it bratwurst?"

"Bratwurst is a wienie," Tina says. When the waitress comes, Tina acts as intermediary—the woman doesn't hear Al's order for coffee, doesn't understand Neil's turning down the fries that come with his dogs, doesn't know what's in liverwurst. When she's gone, Tina settles herself on the Naugahyde seat like a hen. Already she is a mother, I think. This role is her.

Somehow Tina has it in her head that her father and I don't know one another well enough, so after lunch, when Al wants to visit the aquarium, she complains of swollen ankles and offers to drive Neil around Oak Park to look at Frank Lloyd Wright houses. Her mother, who has absolutely no preference, will join them.

Here Al and I stand at the coral reef tank in which a woman in a wetsuit floats, feeding eels and sharks while narrating through a microphone. Her words make bubbles around her head. The aquarium is ancient and dark, so dark that a sign by the entrance warns of pickpockets and purse-snatchers. Thursday is free day and the place is full of small children and exhausted dowdy teachers. Children, now that I am about to become the parent of one, interest me more than the fish.

"I'm really more of a freshwater man, myself," Al admits, after we have stood before the feeding show for a while.

Freshwater fish are not as popular with the kids, and we stroll peaceably through trout and bass and crappie. Being with Tina's father is a little like being with Tina. He follows along, only occasionally commenting, really more a shadow than a firm presence. A couple of times he surprises me by being right beside me when I think I've left him a few tanks back. If it were Tina, she'd once in a while put her fingers in my back pocket, just making sure I knew she was still there.

After seeing everything there is to see, we sit in the foyer with our legs stuck out in front of us, Al's ankles crossed. "Well, I enjoyed that," Al says. "I came here once during the war. It's funny, but I didn't remember until we got here. Then it all came back."

"It's a nice place," I say. The darkness of it is agreeable, very unlike other public buildings, with their depressing fluorescent light.

"Sightseeing was Friday afternoons, our only free time. Every other day, every night, we were on a routine. It's not as bad a thing as you might think, mindless activity."

Not sure how philosophical he means to be, I simply nod.

"Three things," he says, holding up the same number of fingers. "We marched the pier? Well then, you keep your eyes on that guy in front of you, watch the little hairs on his neck. We drank? No brawls, no frenzied bits. A good navy drunk never lets his liquor show. Getting cocky? Well sir, you are not the boss. You are not the big guy anymore."

Again I nod, this time uneasy. Like the bubbles from the woman in the coral reef tank, his anger comes up randomly and in isolated pieces.

He breathes deeply, leveling. "This is a beautiful building. I'm sure Neil could regale us with some interesting structural data, but I'd just as soon not know."

My laugh is hearty and relieved. Tina wants us to be closer? This is close enough.

"You know," says Al, "I think I've quit going fishing. I can't remember the last time I went."

"Last summer?"

"No. No, last summer we stayed at home most the time." It was the summer after Gwen's death. Tina and I had stayed home most of the time, too. Except that isn't quite true either. We went out to distract ourselves, but so much followed us that we seemed to be enclosed by familiar walls all the time, home or not.

"Maybe I fished the Niangua once last spring." Al uncrosses his ankles and lets his feet splay. "I throw everything back anyway. Not that that's any reason not to fish."

Al had written a column a full year after Gwen's death

about teaching her: to walk, to bat, to type. To drive. Though not a motorcycle. Those had been forbidden, Al having posted the statistics for fatalities on the family's refrigerator. She hadn't even been wearing a helmet. I try to imagine a father's anguish on this small but important point, but I can hardly picture Tina and me having a baby at all, let alone a child with a full-fledged will of her own.

"You think of names for the baby?" Al asks me, startling me with the proximity of his thoughts to my own.

"A few. Nothing definite. We're leaning toward Samuel. Or Lily," I add, "if it's a girl."

"Solomon," he says with a snort, shaking his head. "I had kids late," he adds. "I was forty when Tina was born. Somehow people convinced me that having kids young was settling. That was a bad word in my crowd then, *settling*. It meant you weren't going to go to Europe or jazz around here—something like that. So we waited. Not that we went to Paris or anything. We just didn't *settle*. You can't imagine how foolish I felt later. You probably already know this stuff, huh? You been to Paris?"

"Nope." My friends were on Fulbrights, in the Peace Corps, slumming from one lectureship to another, still living with people instead of getting married.

"The most dangerous thing in the world is to have a kid," Al says. "Paris? Hah!" He pulls his legs under him and crosses his arms, nods his head in defiance of some unknown thing. "Maybe we can find today's *New York Times*, you think?"

Ugly as it is, the Falcon is a welcome sight as it rounds the Aquarium driveway. Neil has reclined lengthwise across the backseat to take a nap; I can see his big feet. Tina parks and gets out to stretch. For a moment she doesn't look pregnant, just fully arched backward, fists raised like a child. For that same moment I would like to reclaim our pre-pregnant life. It's not quite panic I experience, there on the bowed marble stairs of the Shedd Aquarium, but when Tina lowers her arms and balloons forward again I lift my heel and step backward up a step instead of down. Practically involuntary. Al turns at my hesitation. What can I look like to him? Someone backing out? Someone unclear about "settling"?

"I like the skyline from here," I say, weak and hardly convincing. I point vaguely toward downtown, stepping forward once more.

We wander the downtown Marshall Field's looking at baby furniture, waiting for Tina's family's visit to be over. Their plane leaves this evening. Their luggage already is nestled tightly in the Falcon's trunk. Though there should be joy in this visit, in our shopping for baby things, for me there is only a sort of shame, not unlike the embarrassment I feel in Tina's being pregnant. Tina once tried to explain this embarrassment to me. She said, "Being pregnant is like walking around saying, 'We fuck.'"

Walking around here buying musical mobiles and layette sets and wrist rattles, I think, is like saying, "Nothing can happen."

We have reservations for dinner at the Hancock Building.

"Here we are," Tina says, spreading her arms like Jimmy Durante as the elevator doors open onto the plush dining room. "Top of the Cock."

Neil sits by the window and names all the buildings one more time for us. The white-yellow almost-spring sun setting behind the clouds reminds me of flights west, when I was a teenager traveling to the beach, where I would take acid and surf all night. I often fantasize, asking the eternal questions: What should I have done? Or, When was I closest to death? One night, so high I couldn't distinguish the shore, fighting a riptide, I felt so sure I would die I struck bargains. Looking now at Al, who sits across from me, I try to communicate some message. *You rode in a bomb bay.* One sentence should do it, but which one? *Fragility and durability are equal.* Al is forever cautioning his children, "Don't play the fool," and I would like to switch the wording, somehow make clear what I feel. *You have a right to play the fool.* But, thinking of Tina, of our own unborn child, I ask instead, *How dare you play the fool?*

I look around me at my in-laws' faces. They are a perfectly ordinary group whom I have grown to love extraordinarily. My sympathy for them is a great maroon warmth in my torso. I open my mouth, looking once more at the setting sun, and almost say that being here reminds me of being in an airplane, but catch myself just in time. We have the whole trip to the airport to discuss flying. Lois looks toward Gary, Indiana. "North?" she says, hopefully.

"South," I tell her.

"Maybe we can see Tower Hall from here," Tina says, leaning over Neil to look down.

Al perks a little at the thought, but after a few minutes of searching, tracing a path with his eyes from Navy Pier to Rush Street, gives up once more. "They blasted it," he says. "It wasn't much to see anyway. Just a dorm for a bunch of navy bums."

"But . . . " Tina begins, doesn't finish.

On the way to the airport, Lois and I again share the back-seat. Into the red dark we drive, Neil donning his glasses to read street signs for Tina.

"Magnolia Street," Lois says dreamily, next to me. "My grandparents used to live there and I would visit in the summers. I rode the train from Kansas City. Sometimes I rode between the cars, until one of the porters would come yell at me."

"That reminds me of riding the El last week," Tina says. "These fourteen-year-old girls getting between the cars and sticking their arms out. I kept thinking, their mothers were pregnant and then had them and then took such good care of them and this is what they do. It pissed me off."

Al stares fiercely out his passenger window.

Lois looks at the backs of her husband's and her daughter's heads, thoughtfully. Not three blocks later we drive past Magnolia Street. I point this out, amazed. "Hey, there it is."

Lois turns to look down it calmly and says, "There's the house, that gray one with the streetlight." She isn't even remotely surprised that at the mere mention of the street it appeared, her grandparents' house along with it. She sits back and smiles, reaching over to pat my hand. Leaving her hand on mine, she watches her grandparents' old neighborhood go by. It isn't much of a neighborhood. Tina always remarks disgustedly on the number of small children allowed near its busy intersections without any adults. But I like it. Guys in spaghetti strap T-shirts are always just hanging around, leaning against a rib place on the corner smoking cigarettes. A little boy lugs an eight-pack of empty returnable Coke bottles into a dark storefront. The local Catholic high school is having some sort of festival, and girls in blue and green plaid skirts go by talking, all defining themselves as individuals as best they can within the dress code—neon lace socks, black boots, spiked hair.

"I'm going to drink the whole way back," Neil says. "Bloody Marys."

"Martinis," Al says. He shakes his head, staring into the distance. "Someone's always telling you how safe it is to fly."

"How is this possible?" Tina asks, after we're home and her family is on their way to Kansas City, braving the skyways once more. "How is it possible that we spend all of today looking for Tower Hall and tonight my mother just happens to remember her grandparents and we just happen to drive right by it? I don't get it." We are in bed, which is where most of her speculations and fears come out, most often just before I am about to drift off. ("Will the baby be normal?" she will ask, rhetorically, and I will always answer, "Yes." "Not a pinhead?" "No.") Annoyed, she punches the pillow that she hugs to herself all night. "Maybe she made it up," Tina says. "I never heard of her grandparents living here. Maybe she just dreamed it up."

But I remember my mother-in-law's hand on mine, her fingers a steady dry warmth. Nothing was going to surprise her anymore.

A few minutes later Tina's thoughts have turned her voice melancholy. She sighs. "I don't think we're going to get over it."

"What's that?"

"Gwen's dying. Our family just isn't going to get over it. Not that that's so bad, but we won't recover, not any one of us and not as a family." She's quiet for a long while, though I can hear her thinking, putting together words. "Maybe we'll name the baby Gwen," she says. "Maybe we'll have a baby who's just like Gwen."

I swallow, try to sound logical, reasonable instead of suddenly and deeply terrified. "No two people can be alike," I say carefully. "Besides, you wouldn't want to have a baby like your sister."

"Yes I would," she says, calm and determined. "You know nothing."

I picture this: a baby lolling in her crib, lazily reaching up to be lifted, loved, her face seductive, teasing. *Love me,* her expression commands. "Except," Tina adds, "I think to have a baby like Gwen we'd need a couple of siblings like me and Neil and a couple of parents like Mom and Dad."

It's all impossibly sad, and I see I am always going to be on the outside anyway, away from the ignition heat of her family. The two of us are our own family, I tell her now and then, when she says "home" and means Kansas City, but even that must remind her that she is really more a member of another, more complex and scarred one, swung through events the two of us have nothing to compare with. This baby was an accident, though Tina's father thinks we are brave to be having it. I imagine him lying in a bomb bay, flying home over the ocean for his father's death. Or Al, standing on the roadway last May, watching any number of bad drivers all maneuver the turn his youngest daughter couldn't make. I reach over now and rest my palm on Tina's tight belly. I can't foresee any future. It gapes before me, before us, terrifying and thrilling. Tina moves my hand a little to the left and presses it with her own palm. Both quiet, we wait to feel a kick.

Slickrock
to Bedrock

Already in McBride's truckbed were two two-men rafts, two two-men tents, three oars, a foot-operated air pump whose bellows was mended with duct tape, four coffin-sized waterproof stuff bags stuffed with clothes and other plastic Zip-Loc bags full of all a child could dream of for playing house and more: bandages, tweezers, moist towelettes, fresh basil, teabags, instant coffee, retractable metal cups, gorp, a deck of cards, crossword puzzle book and pencil, Chapstick, croutons, freeze-dried shrimp creole, freeze-dried vegetarian style tofu burger mix, unlightable waterproof matches, three lighters, *Anna Karenina* (Dart had been reading it since he was a sophomore), marshmallows (the only ones available in Provo's Albertson's were pastel colored), flattened toilet paper (cardboard removed), aspirin, codeine, snake-bite kit, chewing gum (to keep McBride's fingernails out of his mouth), bologna, powdered milk, dry cat food (to feed the fish), tampons, stick cinnamon, toothpaste, Kool-Aid, celluloid sponge, ten packs of Marlboros (Dart's), one pack of Carlton's (Carmel had been smoking one bad cigarette a day since age sixteen), a series of rolled topographical maps of the Dolores River and surrounding area, dried fruit-flavored oatmeal, garbanzos, McBride's thirty-year-old lucky Bulova watch and Carmel's antidepressants (just in case; hidden in a French candy tin).

Forgotten were: Carmel's trashy novels, McBride's condoms, and Dart's spare prescription glasses.

Camping and drinking. McBride, his friend Will Dart, and their friend Carmel, pronounced like Clint Eastwood's town on the Pacific, all on a trip down the Dolores River, rafting the winter's runoff, Slickrock to Bedrock.

The guidebooks advised running the Dolores from late April through May, possibly early June. It was now June 10. At the put-in point at Slickrock, there were no other rafts, and only a few oblique signs of recent human activity: footprints and sunflower seed shells, a red bandana half buried in the silt. By now the river was low enough to have begun clearing from its high-water muddiness, still opaque, but more reminiscent of hazel eyes. It was low enough to bump up against its own rock bottom, riffling the surface.

At sunset, already drunk, Dart stood knee deep a few feet from shore, hand shielding his eyes. He saw cottonwoods, felt the looming invisible promise of canyons downstream. The world seemed a long floating journey, open before him like a promise. Even if he weren't drunk, he reasoned, he would feel this ecstasy, this conviction that if he simply lifted his feet he would float away upright, that the water would greet him as easily as it would a piece of driftwood, coddling him along until it found him a home. The face he turned to his friends—Carmel squatting in the sand to find a skipping stone, pragmatic frowning McBride already unloading the truck—was as contained as Dart could make it. His heart had filled his chest cavity; his body had some keen affinity for this place that he had no control over. These yearly trips were like returning to childhood for Dart; he could almost feel as if he had no history—no failed courses, no demeaning jobs, no ex-girlfriends, no disappointed parents. Here, now, he felt powerful enough to discover something, a comet, for instance, or a new species of insect, as if this optimism was wholly fresh and portentous instead of annual and transient.

McBride threw gear from the truckbed, swinging and releasing in an invigorating rhythm while the stuff bags landed with soft thuds on the sand. Soon, of course, all would be chaos and muck, but for now there was a sense of plentitude and order, as if they'd descended into a well-stocked bomb shelter.

Tonight they would camp here, McBride decided, then put in early tomorrow. Their stretch was forty-five river miles and he'd told the sheep farmer at Bedrock they'd be taking out in three days, which meant fifteen miles tomorrow. McBride wasn't as comfortable in the water as he was on a trail. Every year there was at least one moment when he panicked in the water. He was always in favor of portaging around the most dangerous rapids; every year they rafted over anyway. McBride managed always to be in the second raft so that he could watch Dart in the first one find the river's tongue and ride it out. Then he would follow. Or, if Dart blew it, well, McBride had the advantage of that nonexample also.

But that was tomorrow's anxiety. Today he was happy unloading, knowing tonight they would be right here. He didn't have to worry yet about boulders and undercurrents and those deep black whirling holes that sucked their tiny rafts like toy boats in a draining bathtub. Guidebooks talked about the easiness of the Dolores, but the lower the water got, the less easy it truly was. McBride paused for a moment to look at the river at twilight. It was beautiful, even with Dart flailing in it, and McBride was peaceful, contemplating dinner, scanning the sand for a flat tent space.

In their established division of labor, Carmel built fires. She had a knack. Looking for kindling, she considered her ingenuity at destruction: burning things up, knocking things down, killing things off. The flawless man she'd left in Salt Lake City told her to come back when her ego felt better, when she could begin loving herself. Before then, she'd be nothing but trouble to them both. He saw her little sabotages in their relationship as self-hate; she saw them as extensions of the same destructive impulses that had snipped spiders' legs from their bodies or that had sucker-punched her brothers when she was younger. Simple love of conflict and fury and bang-bang. She'd brought a gun with her last year and shot a fat whistling pig on a rock ledge. Dart had been appalled; McBride, merely startled. She left the gun at home this time.

Still, it was her intention this year to poach a sheep; without a gun, it would be more difficult, but so much the better. There was a pasture they passed tomorrow. Camp was only a mile or so beyond. They could double back in the night. McBride (it had to be McBride; Dart was too soft) would help. Maybe they would drown the sheep.

Carmel's pleasure in these trips, this the seventh one, had dwindled. Their first had been when she was seventeen, going rafting with her best friend, the best friend's older brother, and his friend McBride. Four of them, she and Dart in the slow-leak raft because they were the thinnest, hefty McBride and Dart's chunky sister Lana Dart in the fully inflated model, navigating the then-unknown Dolores. The first time it was an adventure; every time since had been anticlimactic for Carmel. She'd destroyed her friendship with Lana, so the next year Lana hadn't wanted to come. The year after that she'd decided she'd fallen in love with Dart, but then realized she really hadn't by the end of the trip, which kept them at odds for most of the following year. Anyway, the point was, every year on the Dolores made Carmel realize she'd been better off the year before.

This time, for instance, she'd told her boyfriend Lawrence that she was going rafting, as she always did the first part of June, and then didn't even explain why she wasn't inviting him. Maybe he would have understood; it was hard to say, but she so badly didn't want him along that she didn't chance it.

"Someday," Lawrence told her as she knelt mashing her down bag in its preposterously small sack, "you will spontaneously combust. Poof! Nothing left but shoes and the silver from your teeth."

That night in the tent they'd designated the boys', Will Dart lay in his bag lazily masturbating and considering becoming a hermit. But I *like* people, he kept remembering. Beside him McBride snored out such strong alcoholic vapors that Dart wanted to light an experimental match over his face. Dart himself was so drunk he didn't think it would be possible to get anywhere with his hands. Still, it felt great to be on the Dolores again, and this was his private celebration.

Seeing Carmel had also excited him. He'd been in love with her since he first met her, back when she'd been friends with his sister. He despaired when he thought of Lana, how ordinary she'd become, how narrow her vision and aspirations. He'd been flattered to discover Carmel still laughed at his jokes, still was the good sport he'd left off in Salt Lake at the end of last year's trip. She and he had had a near-miss sort of messy almost-relationship which now and then seemed to get in the way of solid friendship, but he'd watched closely and was relieved to see she seemed to have put it all behind her. She would be good for Lana, he decided, if Lana would only allow her in.

Listening to the water outside, Dart imagined that he and McBride and Carmel might just raft past their take-out point in a few days, continue down the Dolores until it emptied into the Colorado, then keep right on going into an exotic outdoor future, which, though clear in his mind, he knew had no reality. Tree houses, rope swings, log cabins, spring water, cords and cords of chopped wood, a continuous campfire. Unrealistic, but pleasurable nonetheless, so much so that he quieted his hands and simply lay still, reveling in his utopia.

McBride woke with a strictly camper's hangover, sore not only in the head and stomach but in all major joints and muscles, particularly the back. He'd thrown himself on his bag last night without clearing the ground beneath him of rocks he'd missed when he first set up the tent. But if camper's hangovers were the worst kind, they were also the shortest-lived.

Oddly, Carmel was already awake when McBride crawled from the tent. Dart slept the deep sleep of the afternoon riser, but there was Carmel, also usually a late sleeper, sitting on a rock at the river's edge smoking a cigarette and drinking coffee. A fire, whose smoke probably had wakened him, burned weakly in last night's ashes. McBride and Carmel corresponded during the year, occasionally making vague plans to meet halfway between Salt Lake and Missoula, where McBride lived, but never quite pulling it off. Still, they were friends, and it struck him for the first time that she was not happy. He tried to think if she had ever been happy, if he'd been so obtuse all these years as to have missed what now seemed very obvious. Yes, he decided, she'd been happy before, maybe even as recently as last summer, but was no longer. It was somehow nakedly obvious to him in her hunched back and stringy hair.

"Morning," he said to her, hands in his pockets.

"Hey," Carmel answered. "You know, I was just thinking we've got to transfer all that booze to plastic bottles."

"I was thinking that, too," McBride said, grateful she was not going to get weepy on him. Every year he fell a little bit in love with Carmel and those feelings accumulated, making him fonder of her now than he ever had been.

Carmel spotted a sheep in the late morning. She and Dart shared the less leaky of the rafts while McBride and two-thirds of the gear rode behind. The sun was brilliant and Carmel had taken off her workshirt and tied it scarflike around her chest. She then reclined sideways in the boat to sunbathe, allowing Dart to row happily along. She only rowed over rapids. It was an arrangement they'd come up with years ago, one that Carmel knew would offend McBride's sense of fair play, but one that Dart seemed completely content with.

"Sheep!" she told Dart, rocking the raft in her struggle to sit upright.

"Hey, bubba," Dart yelled out to a stupefied animal, who watched them listlessly.

"Your days are numbered," Carmel warned it.

The river was wide here, sprawled luxuriously in the midst of farmland. It would narrow soon, be pushed too quickly through the enclosing sandstone canyon walls, but for now it was lazy, shallow, and broad.

Carmel felt the same way. "I forgot my books," she told Dart. "I was going to bring a frothy romance to read to you today." She reclined again.

"I brought *Anna*," Dart offered.

"No way. Only fluff on the Dolores." Carmel opened her eyes long enough to watch Dart smile, light another cigarette in the chain he had going, and readjust his glasses. They were tied to his head with a piece of rope. Every year she meant to buy him a strap designed for the same purpose and every year she forgot. It occurred to her that she could tell McBride to bring it for her next year and he would not let her down. She looked beyond Dart to the rear raft, where McBride paddled three times on the left, then three on the right, cutting a fairly straight line, which did not even approximate the wobbly course Dart had the two of them on. Taking hits on his cigarette seemed to get in the way. But there was McBride with his trimmed beard and broad shoulders and khaki outdoorsman shirt, at work on the river. Perhaps she should fall in love with him, perhaps he would be the steady and firm hand she might just now need.

"Look at him," Carmel said to Dart.

Dart raised his cigarette to McBride and grinned. "What ho?" he yelled back, but McBride only nodded, busy rowing. His mind was too one-tracked, Carmel decided. She couldn't possibly fall in love with him.

"He thinks I think I'm Cleopatra," she told Dart.

"Aren't you?" he grinned again.

Carmel had the sudden temptation to make him unhappy. People could become too smugly gleeful for her taste. "I should have brought my gun," she said, watching his face.

Dart's smile turned to bewilderment. He was a child, she saw, whose feelings not only could be hurt but were always right there on the surface, susceptible. "What for?" he asked.

Carmel's desire to hurt him vanished. She would have given him a kiss on the cheek if that were possible, but, instead, only laughed. "Just kidding." Why, Carmel wondered, was Dart not right for her? In anyone else, thin shoulders and thick glasses would not have put her off; she'd dated that physical type before. But the one time she'd been able to love him he'd been too shy in responding, too slow to seduce, asking her permission every step of the way. Embarrassment for him rekindled in her when she remembered his asking if it was all right to kiss her. Embarrassment and a specific kind of anger she had for people weaker than herself.

It was noon when they came upon their traditional first campsite, an idyllic spot just before the big canyons, where they set their tents beneath trees. Though hundreds of rafters must have camped here, the site remained pristine enough to make McBride believe no one had been there since them, one year earlier. In all the rivers he'd rafted, all the trails he'd hiked, there was never a place quite like the Dolores, whose devotees seemed intent on maintaining its wildness. The stretch starting tomorrow had nothing human in it, past or present: no phone wires, no roads, no rusty cans, no fences, no old mining sites: nothing but their toy boats. Tomorrow's campsite was under the shelf of a rock wall in which there were hundreds of little naturally occurring holes. Every year Carmel would find stones to put in the holes, filling a few rows before they left. Every year her stones were still there, the only real indication some person had been at work in paradise.

McBride glided to a clean stop after watching Dart and Carmel's sloppy one. Carmel was hanging onto brush while Dart clambered up the side, kicking mud in behind him. McBride steadied his raft with an oar set in the shallows and then stepped gingerly up a lesser incline a few yards down from his friends. Only his left foot got wet, and only the sole at that.

"Lunch time," Carmel pronounced. Thin as she was, she was a voracious eater. It was she who always made them bring along provisions such as marshmallows and bologna.

After lunch, Dart wanted to hike and McBride decided to go with him. The two of them couldn't get Carmel to budge from her spot beneath a tree. "I'll read," she said. "I'll drink." McBride looked over his shoulder a few times as they left her, but she hadn't moved to dig out a book, hadn't gotten a drink. She watched the river.

She was still watching when they returned a few hours later. McBride worried until he saw that she'd set up both tents and found firewood. There was a big pit set with twigs and kindling, a blanket beside it, an aluminum pot full of water, and the makings for shrimp creole laid out.

They waited for dark, drinking Kool-Aid and rum. McBride had tried to fix freeze-dried food in his kitchen in Missoula, but it never tasted even remotely like it did on the river. He ate heartily tonight, ignoring the tiny black flecks of ash.

"Found a great spring," Dart told Carmel. "Beautiful."

She nodded. McBride noticed she'd almost finished a bottle of rum while they were gone, but was not her usual boisterous drunk self. Preoccupied, she smiled at their jokes while seeming to wish she were elsewhere. McBride found himself reaching too hard for the funny lines, checking her expression frequently, waiting for approval.

They sang cowboy songs around the red late-night coals, Dart and Carmel passing joints between them. McBride only risked getting high when his self-confidence was up; otherwise, he became impossibly paranoid, struck dumb by the realization of all his inadequacies. Dart and Carmel did not share this problem. Soon, Dart had to call it a night. His eyes, in the camplight, had retreated. Rowing, hiking, boozing, doping. He didn't bother getting to the tent, just wrapped himself in his sleeping bag too close to the fire.

McBride could have slept then, too, but Carmel worried him and he decided to wait. After a moment she stood, surprisingly well balanced, and, with her boot toe, rolled Dart away from the fire. When she sat down, it was very near to McBride, whose cheeks flushed at her proximity. He could see a hair growing on her chin.

"Listen," she said in her husky voice. "You like mutton?"

McBride listened while she explained an outrageous plan to kill a sheep. Apparently, she'd been thinking about it all day. She wanted to rope the animal's ankles like a rodeo rider, then level a blow to its head. McBride was too stunned to answer when she finished.

Finally, he said, "What rope?"

"We'll use my belt."

"You don't want to hurt a lamb."

"Yes," she said calmly. "I really do. We just have to get back upriver. It's not like we wouldn't eat it," she told McBride. "You guys fish, right? What's the big difference? You think a fuzzy live thing has more rights than a slimy one?" She looked at him with grim amusement. "If you don't come," she said, "I'll do it by myself."

The boat was cold and strange in the dark and the river seemed four times as deep. The canyon downstream beckoned to them like a void. They rowed furiously against the current, moving slowly but steadily. McBride's exhausted muscles, lubricated with liquor, performed without his thinking about them. He didn't believe they'd find any sheep, but Carmel's bloodthirstiness was disturbing enough on its own. He couldn't imagine how it would seem when he was sober.

"No sheep," McBride said gratefully, when they reached the pasture. Carmel grabbed a handful of brush and pulled them ashore.

"We can find them," she said. True, the moon was sufficiently bright to see landmarks—trees, the biggest of the rocks in the river. But beyond a certain point in the pasture there was nothing but shadow, a tree line, or distant row of hay.

"This is ridiculous," McBride said after they'd tied the raft to a clump of willows and begun making their way through the field.

Carmel kept thinking she could hear them, just over there, just beyond. But the sheep seemed wilier than she had imagined. Their elusiveness only made her more certain in her desire to kill one; they were fairer game than she'd previously believed. They zigzagged across a rocky field making sheep noises, McBride still a little drunk. Carmel, on the other hand, didn't feel a thing, not intoxicated, not high, not tired. Only mad. Furious. Her disappointment had grown into a terrible anger. She began throwing rocks, trying at first to hit things, then just pitching them one after another ahead of her. No fucking sheep.

But it wasn't just sheep. It was everything, big and small. It was the chill in the air and the slightly tight corduroys she wore. It was her. It was her boyfriend Lawrence and her men friends McBride and Dart. Not one of them knew her, really knew her. Sometimes she thought Lawrence understood the real her. Then there were times, like today on the river, when it seemed only Will Dart could know her. They all knew parts of her. But she couldn't be everything around any one of them. She missed having women friends. She missed Lana Dart. Always she was screwing things up. Friendships, romances— when they went awry, the fault was hers.

Next to her, McBride pulled out a pack of gum and offered her a stick. With effort, she was polite. "No, thank you." Her contempt for him was very high. What kind of man was he, trailing her around on this chase? He seemed to find it all very anecdotal. He would tell the Story of the Sheep Hunt some day, Carmel thought. The Story of Crazy Carmel. She began running.

The night opened ahead of her, tripping her but not spilling her. McBride was calling her name. He would wait. He would wait all night, if she made him. Her men were, one and all, loyal. Loyal to a fault. She forced herself to run harder, faster, stumbling as she went but not falling. What kept her from falling? To think about falling was to make it impossible. She ran until she was hurting everywhere—cheeks, lungs, thighs, toes. She wanted to hurt more. She wanted to be unconscious in pain. Her fury then reached its apex and, headfirst, she plunged herself down.

Dart woke practically lying in the warm ashes of last night's fire. When he opened his eyes he felt lousy, but with them closed he was okay. "Coffee," he said aloud. He'd expected one or both of the others to be up by now, waiting to laugh at him; he was usually the last. But the tent flaps were tied down and all of yesterday's clutter seemed untouched. He decided to skinny-dip.

Sitting on an upturned raft, he stripped, checking as he went for ticks. The sun, just now cresting the trees, caused a wave of goose bumps on his pale skin. The Dolores was snow runoff, just barely above freezing, and there was no good place to ease in slowly. Dart dipped his long ugly feet in first, then delicately leaped in up to his waist, biting back a scream as cold jolted through him. It took ages too long to scramble out.

But as big a shock as the water had been, the sight of Carmel standing near the stuff bags was a bigger one. She looked as if she'd been mauled by a bear. Even without his glasses, Dart could see scrapes running the length of her jawline, both of her black eyes, the puffy mass of her mouth. She hadn't seen him, though he wasn't very far away. She was searching through a bag, gingerly pulling things out and dropping them to the ground. Dart dressed rapidly, his heartbeat rampant.

"What happened?" he asked, hating the breathlessness in his voice.

She gave him an indifferent appraisal, bare feet to wet head, and shook a metal candy tin. "I tripped."

The whole morning went like that. Dart felt as if he must have insulted somebody's mother in his sleep or committed some similar unforgivable blunder. All of a sudden he was in the supply raft by himself while McBride went ahead with Carmel. Carmel was rowing, besides. He tried to be angry, as he believed was justified, but all he felt was ashamed. He'd failed, though for the life of him he couldn't figure out how.

When they entered the beginning of the maze that was the canyons, he found himself not paying particularly close attention to the water; instead, he was watching McBride and Carmel, looking for signs they were lovers. That had happened before, two friends began sleeping together and didn't bother to tell him until he'd made a fool of himself, so he tried to tactfully accept the new situation like a good third wheel. He tried to remember that the Dolores was the important part: the beautiful canyons whose high smooth walls arched up on either side of him. Black deposits in the sandstone ran down the terra-cotta like spilled paint, tapering at the base. He saw a bald eagle, wings spread, gliding on a thermal, and nearly lost himself in the wonder of it. Nearly. Overwhelming scenery or no, Dart was unable to let go. He smoked and paddled and looked about in awe, but all he could see was the tiny boat ahead of him and his two friends.

Since McBride was such an efficient oarsman, they got far ahead, soon completely out of sight. Dart made miscalculations, took the wrong tongue over a rock, touched bottom. Water accumulated in the boat after every rapids. And, for the first time in seven years, he capsized.

He'd decided to circumvent a large flat rock which the

water flowed smoothly over. Sometimes you could raft such a rock, making a small leap so you didn't get caught in the undertow on the other side. But his confidence in doing this was shaken today and he chose the narrow stream of water to the left, needing to quickly bear even farther left to avoid the shallows just beyond. Halfway through, he saw that the rock jutted under the path he'd taken as well and that its shape pulled everything to the right, regardless. The correct path was over, and he'd gone around. His raft seemed to be sucked straight down, its vinyl floor pulling away from his feet and the sides narrowing around him. He lost his glasses. There was nothing but foam. White foam and suction. The thrill of being removed entirely from his raft was exhilarating and Dart actually came up laughing with fright. He didn't notice how cold it was until he was past the undertow, casting about for his broken oar.

Carmel and McBride were gone. Everything was floating downstream—red stuff bags and loose clothing, the raft itself, two oar pieces. Flotsam, he thought. His glasses had sunk. Dart stood shivering in the shallows of a sandbar and hoped his friends would think he'd drowned. With a great sadness he realized this was the last year on the Dolores. He didn't usually recognize the moments in his life when it fell apart, but he thought that right now was an exception.

He sighed, still shaken by his capsizing. McBride and Carmel would have to retrieve the supplies themselves. He was going to sit down and dry out, have a little rest.

McBride kept thinking, *Everything has changed.* He rowed distractedly, not speaking to Carmel, just concentrating on her oar ahead of his, watching the water drip off it as she lifted it from the river, over and over. *Everything has changed.*

They'd spent the night at the pasture, McBride holding her

until she finally slept. There was blood on his sleeves, blood in his beard. She'd been incoherent, ranting, then clinging, still trying to hurt herself, scraping her bare hands on rocks. At daybreak they'd returned to camp. He'd understood she didn't want to ride with Dart today.

"You better?" he'd asked that morning.

"Than what?" she'd answered, wryly.

They reached their traditional campsite at Bull Spring much earlier than normal. It hadn't been the usual second day of running the rapids and playing Capture the Flag with each other. Carmel had seemed in a hurry and McBride was willing to accommodate her. It seemed she might be capable of anything.

When he saw Dart's raft and the gear float by camp, his throat constricted. He realized he was looking for Dart among it. There was nowhere to get help, nowhere. They were hours from any kind of phone or town.

"I have to go back upstream," McBride told Carmel. Her eyes were wide and empty. "Maybe you can try to get the supplies?" She looked blankly downstream as two of the stuff bags rounded a bend. The raft had caught in the rocks, along with a third red bag. Carmel nodded.

McBride found himself paddling against the current for the second day in a row. How stupid to let Dart get so far behind. But he'd been sulking, McBride thought, sulking and falling behind. McBride vowed that he'd tell Dart everything, all of Carmel's ramblings and tears, if only he were okay.

The Dolores had never seemed to McBride to be a deadly river. Intimidating at times, threatening, but not deadly. That was an important distinction. Of course, the river itself was not the problem. It was the people. What made everyone so unreliable? McBride couldn't think of one time he'd ever been as transparent to another human as Carmel had been to him last night, as out of control. He didn't like the feeling it gave him, power and embarrassment and empathy and pity, all at once. He shook his head.

He tried to imagine Carmel's life in Salt Lake City, but found himself drawing all his knowledge about her from the week he spent with her annually. Which could hardly be called her life. He had visited her once in college in Colorado. Just dropped in unexpectedly. Her reaction was not what he had expected. She'd opened her dorm room door and stared at him for a moment before she'd let him in. Photographs filled her allotted half of the wall space, and in every picture people were smiling. He'd commented on this and she'd told him that in her photographs people smiled; otherwise, they didn't get their picture taken. The faces were eerie and soon McBride saw that smiling was just a way of being nice about baring your teeth.

He thought it ironic that Carmel had become a nurse; he couldn't think of anyone dedicated to less healthy habits. But in his mind, when he put her in a white uniform and sensible white shoes, she was no longer Carmel. Carmel was the woman who last year had lain, hands behind her head, with him and Will Dart on a huge flat rock and watched the moon rise above the canyon walls. Today, he felt that woman had disappeared.

"I'm a parasite," she'd told him. "I get in people and make them sick." She rammed her head into McBride's chest. "Sometimes I think I'm a public contagion, like these cultures at the hospital. Hazards to the general populace. Just like that."

How did you respond? McBride wondered, though it didn't seem to matter.

"I could kill someone," Carmel whispered, last night and right now, in McBride's ear. "I could do it."

He saw Will Dart standing on a sandbar. He rowed more furiously, his eyes tearing in relief. Dart's glasses were gone, his clothing was soaked. A rivulet of blood ran down one calf until it dried at his ankle. His thick black hair stood on end like a fright wig. But there he was, waving his gangly arms and smiling. "What ho?"

Carmel was so happy to see Dart come back alive, she started crying. She'd managed to drag in one of the stuff bags and the raft, which was completely deflated.

"Hey," she said to him, coughing. "I saved the bag with the tequila and the B&B. I knew you'd be glad."

"Good work," Dart said. His eyes, without his glasses, wandered a little. When he looked at Carmel, they skidded to the right, as if she'd moved, then centered again.

"We're a sight," she told him, suddenly happier than she had been in months. They were messy but safe, warm in the sunlight and out of any danger in the water. There would be a fire. They would drink and laugh and sleep underneath the blanket that had made it. Carmel wished suddenly that McBride had some wounds as well. His stern expression reminded her that he'd been the one to rescue both her and Dart. He was humorless as a martyr when he came away from Dart's bedraggled raft.

"Holey?" Dart asked, smiling weakly.

"Ruined," McBride answered without smiling. "And a full day from Bedrock, too. Jesus."

Carmel thought he was being melodramatic. "We can squish together in the other one," she said, then remembered last night, when *he'd* indulged *her* theatrics. She wished she could erase the night, erase her long complicated confessional session with him. Now when he looked at her, he seemed to think he understood something, that he had witnessed her bared soul. Stupid, she thought. He didn't know her at all. In fact, battered and dense Dart seemed closer to her now.

"Let me clean your cuts," Carmel said to him.

McBride tried to catch her eye, but she wouldn't let him. Fuck him, she thought, leading Dart to the warm sand beneath a rock ledge. She dabbed her shirttail in a capful of tequila and swabbed his knees.

"Pretty incredible undertow," he said, wincing.

"Yeah?"

"Oh yeah. You wouldn't think the Dolores ever got that deep, but I couldn't feel bottom."

"Huh." She sat back and touched her own scrapes. "I wiped out on a rock," she explained shyly. "Literally." How necessary it had seemed last night, how foolish now.

"Maybe we should have some shots of this," Dart said, swirling the bottle.

"No limes," Carmel said.

"Emergency substitution?"

"Toothpaste." They laughed, each took a shot with a dallop of Crest afterwards to kill the bite. They sat getting drunk while McBride found firewood and tried to patch the raft with first-aid tape. Carmel began absently filling the little holes in the wall behind her. Her work from the last seven years was still untouched. The holes reminded her of a miniature city of ancient cliff dwellings. In the beginning, she sort of thought of her pebbles as inhabitants, but now she just thought of them as rocks, clogging the spaces.

Dart joined her and before long Carmel curled up on the warm sand and just watched him, content and sleepy. She fell into a dreamless sleep.

She looked like hell, McBride thought, but they both wanted her anyway. He couldn't explain it, but he wanted des-

perately to make love to her. His feelings had run the gamut
with her today, pity to anger to passion. Maybe it was all the
same. But he wanted her. He and Will Dart shuffled aimlessly
around camp waiting for her to wake up. Neither wanted to
hike, neither wanted to sit and talk to the other. They waited
for her.

He'd discovered that Dart's raft could hold a fair amount of
air for about fifteen minutes. Then it had to be repumped.
Tomorrow they would stop every mile or so to get the bellows.
Thankfully, he'd put them in the raft with him and Carmel
that morning. Ever since he'd found Dart alive, he'd grown
more and more annoyed with him. What kind of idiot capsized on the Dolores? One of the slowest floating rivers in the
nation, the easiest stretch. And Dart was supposed to be the
expert raftsman.

He looked at the sky, waiting for dark, waiting to light a
fire, waiting for Carmel to rise.

Carmel was hungry when she woke, but all their carefully
packed, waterproofed food had floated away, spices and all. So
much preparation quickly rendered moot.

They drank B&B out of the bailing cup, eyeing each other. It
began to scare her. No one was stopping it, Carmel thought.
No one made a move to stop what was going to happen.

When it got dark, Carmel stood and walked out of the fire's
light. She stopped when she was far enough away that they
could not see her but she could see them. Who would come
after her? she wondered. Dutiful McBride? Pathetic Dart?

She watched as they sat on either side of the fire, good
friends whom she had set at odds with one another. For a
fleeting moment, she savored her destruction of their friendship. Then she dug her fingernails into her forearms and bit
her lower lip. Her own dismal unhappiness made her want to

infect everyone around her, and yet it was a vicious circle: causing pain was what she hated in herself. When does it end? she wondered.

Dart stood up at the fire, stretched his long bruised arms over his head. He said something to McBride, who didn't look up and didn't answer. "I guess I'll go find her," or something else as equally euphemistic. He came toward her with unflagging efficiency, straight to her. "Can I sit?" he whispered, asking permission.

She nodded, irritated. As soon as he sat, she grabbed him and kissed his face, over and over, pressing her sore lips ferociously against his soft features—all this before he could begin his own awkward dumb way of doing the same thing.

"Unzip," she commanded. He was hard, and they were fast.

"McBride!" Carmel yelled, before Dart had a chance to gather his wits. He struggled to rise, pulling his sandy pants up as he went, catching pubic hair when he zipped. "McBride, come here!" What was she doing?

Dart watched as Carmel, completely nude, met McBride halfway between the fire's light and the blackness outside of it. McBride apparently had been walking blind for a few yards because his face, when he finally saw her, went slack. She wanted to have sex right there, Dart saw. She embraced McBride, who stood without moving, lifting one naked thigh to his belt, nuzzling his throat. McBride said something as he tried to push her away. Carmel laughed, then said, ". . . fuck . . . " *Fuck Dart?* Dart wondered. *I want to fuck you!* She jumped against McBride, forcing him to cup his hands around her buttocks to keep her from falling. He kissed her. Dart could see their heads turning in a long, if not passionate, then painful, kiss. His stomach churned—humiliation, shame, self-pity.

To be inside her had been wonderful. He hadn't ever really allowed himself the full fantasy of sex with Carmel. But years of suspense had made it immeasurably spectacular. Dart found himself stirred again by the memory, despite what he saw before him, McBride staggering toward the blanket near the fire with Carmel in his arms. They would make love. He would watch. It all happened as if he were imagining it and not actually witnessing it, McBride's muscular body in the firelight, Carmel's savage face over his shoulder, McBride crying out and Dart feeling it as if it were himself.

Then he heard his name. Carmel raised her hands to her mouth and yelled his name into the night, over the sound of the water. He would join them, he realized, he would walk to the fire, he would undress, he would be a willing part of whatever this was, hypnotized but conscious, and he did, *doing* it at the precise moment he could *imagine* it, as if there were no difference between the two.

The farmer, as was previously arranged, had parked McBride's truck near the takeout point. The farmer's sheep, curious and stupid, slow and smelly, milled about it. McBride paid him ten dollars and got behind the wheel. He couldn't believe how great it felt to steer, to start the engine and feel the motor respond to his foot on the pedal.

There'd been no discussion that day as they leapfrogged to Bedrock, stopping three or four times an hour to pump air into the raft. The thing was, there was no one to blame, McBride realized, no one to think worse of than the other two. They would never see one another again, it was clear. There was something freeing about it, something poisonous.

Aimed toward Nucla, clouds on the far horizon bubbling up behind one another like an H-bomb blast, Carmel introduced the peach schnapps from her pack, the last of their two-hundred-dollar cache. She sat between the men in the truck and McBride guessed they'd gotten used to her scabbed face: he couldn't make out the awfulness in it anymore. She waved her bottle by the throat across Dart and out the window. Once it was empty, she let loose. It smashed onto the pavement behind them. "Happy flat fucking tires, assholes!" she yelled.

They were looking for liquor when they passed a farm. Dart wondered aloud if the children in the yard, three of them playing some odd-looking game, would know how to help. He and Carmel debated this point. Drunk, McBride did not register until the truck was well past the driveway that one of the boys had tied the other to a telephone pole, that the little girl, presumably the boys' sister, was standing by crying, helpless. He presented this evidence to his cohorts, who turned to look out the back window.

"Think he'll get hit by lightning?" Carmel asked, scientifically.

"Should we do something?" Dart said. "Us?"

But the rain began and the fuzz of all that peachiness rubbed and chafed McBride's insides and extremities. He shut his eyes and said to himself, What if I weren't here, driving by at this precise moment? Who, besides me, could save that boy? When he opened them, he was crossing the yellow line and the oval emblem of a Peterbilt was coming at him. "Chicken!!" Carmel screeched happily, and they pushed 85, 90, veering at the last moment, high on not giving one goddamn about it.

Fishtailing, the three of them rode into the storm, lightning striking—Dart told them no, lightning doesn't strike, exactly, it meets its countercurrent from the ground halfway—and trees bowing, rain in sheets breaking over them like waves on a beach, the rhythm of a pulsing heart, blinding them every other beat.